Return
to the
Hundred
Acre Wood

EGMONT

We bring stories to life

First published in Great Britain 2011
by Egmont UK Limited
239 Kensington High Street, London W8 6SA

Text by David Benedictus © Trustees of the Pooh Properties 2011
Illustrations by Mark Burgess © Trustees of the Pooh Properties 2011

Edited by Anna Bowles and Sharika Sharma
Designed by Suzanne Cooper

ISBN 978 1 4052 5160 0

1 3 5 7 9 10 8 6 4 2

www.egmont.co.uk

A CIP catalogue record for this title is available
from The British Library.

Printed in Italy

Return
to the
Hundred
Acre Wood

in which Winnie-the-Pooh enjoys further adventures
with Christopher Robin and his friends

By David Benedictus
based upon the Pooh stories by A.A. Milne
with decorations by Mark Burgess
in the style of E.H. Shepard

DEDICATION

You gave us Christopher Robin and Pooh
And a forest of shadows and streams,
And the whole world smiled with you, as you
                    Offered us your dreams.
I took up the offer and page upon page
And line upon fanciful line,
I tried to show in a different age
                    Your dreams are mine.

EXPOSITION

Pooh and Piglet, Christopher Robin and Eeyore were last seen in the Forest – oh, can it really be eighty years ago? But dreams have a logic of their own and it is as if the eighty years have passed in a day.

Looking over my shoulder, Pooh says: "Eighty is a good number really but it could just as well be eighty weeks or days or minutes as years," and I say: "Let's call it eighty seconds, and then it'll be as though no time has passed at all."

Piglet says: "I tried to count to eighty once, but when I got to thirty-seven the numbers started jumping out at me and turning cartwheels, especially the sixes and nines."

"They do that when you're least expecting it," says Pooh.

"But are you really going to write us new adventures?" Christopher Robin asks. "Because we rather liked the old ones."

"I didn't like the ones with the Heffalumps in," adds Piglet, shuddering.

"And can they end with a little smackerel of something?" asks Pooh, who may have put on a few ounces in eighty years.

"He'll get it wrong," says Eeyore, "see if he doesn't. What does he know about donkeys?"

Of course Eeyore is right, because I don't know; I can only guess. But guessing can be fun too. And if occasionally I think I have guessed right, I shall reward myself with a chocolate biscuit, one of those with chocolate on one side only so you don't get sticky fingers and leave marks on the paper, and if sometimes I am afraid that I have guessed wrong, I shall just have to go without.

"We'll know," says Christopher Robin. "We'll help you get it right, if we can." And Pooh and Piglet smile and nod their heads, but Eeyore says: "Not that you are likely to. Nobody ever does."

D.B.

With acknowledgments to E.H. Shepard,
original illustrator of the Winnie-the-Pooh stories.

The publisher would like to thank
the Trustees of the Pooh Properties Trust and especially
Michael Brown and Peter Janson-Smith who have
long striven to make this book possible and who
have made invaluable suggestions and contributions
at all stages of its development, and also
Janice Swanson of Curtis Brown whose advice
and patience throughout have smoothed the way
and been of the greatest benefit to all concerned.

CONTENTS

·CHAPTER ONE·

in which Christopher Robin returns

W̲HO STARTED IT? Nobody knew. One moment there was the usual Forest babble; the wind in the trees, the crow of a cock, the cheerful water in the streams. Then came the Rumour: Christopher Robin is back!

Owl said he heard it from Rabbit, and Rabbit said he heard it from Piglet, and Piglet said he just sort of heard it, and Kanga said why not ask Winnie-the-Pooh? And since that seemed like a Very Encouraging Idea on such a sunny morning, off Piglet trotted, arriving in time to find Pooh anxiously counting his pots of honey.

"Isn't it odd?" said Pooh.

"Isn't what odd?"

Pooh rubbed his nose with his paw. "I wish they would sit still. They shuffle around when they think I'm not looking. A moment ago there were eleven and now

there are only ten. It is odd, isn't it, Piglet?"

"It's even," said Piglet, "if it's ten, that is. And if it isn't, it isn't." Hearing himself saying this, Piglet thought that it didn't sound quite right, but Pooh was still counting, moving the pots from one corner of the table to the other and back again.

"Bother," said Pooh. "Christopher Robin would know if he was here. He was good at counting. He always made things come out the same way twice and that's what good counting is."

"But Pooh . . ." Piglet began, the tip of his nose growing pink with excitement.

"On the other hand it's not easy to count things when they won't stay still. Like snowflakes and stars."

"But Pooh . . ." And if Piglet's nose was pink before, it was scarlet now.

"I've made up a hum about it. Would you like to hear it, Piglet?"

Piglet was about to say that hums were splendid things, and Pooh's hums were the best there were, but Rumours come first; then he thought what a nice feeling it was to have a Big Piece of News and to be about to Pass It On; then he remembered the hum which Pooh had made up about him, Piglet, and how it had had seven verses, which was more verses than a hum had ever had since time began, and that they were all about him, and so he said: "Ooh, yes, Pooh, please," and Pooh glowed a little because a hum is all very well as far as it goes, and very well indeed when it goes for seven verses, but it isn't a Real Hum until it's been tried out on somebody, and while honey is always welcome, it's welcomest of all directly after a hum.

This is the hum which Pooh hummed to Piglet on the day which started like any other day and became a very special day indeed.

If you want to count your honey,
You must put it in a row,
In the sun if it is sunny,
If it's snowy in the snow.

And you'll know when you have counted
How much honey you have got.
Yes, you'll know what the amount is
And so therefore what it's not.

"And I think it's eleven," added Pooh, "which is an excellent number of pots for a Thursday, though twelve would be even better."

"Pooh," said Piglet quickly, in case there was a third verse on the way which would be nice, but time-consuming, "I have a Very Important Question to ask you."

"The answer is Yes," said Pooh. "It is time for a little something."

"But, Pooh," said Piglet, the tip of his nose by now quite crimson with anxiety and frustration, "the question is not about little somethings but big somethings. It's about Christopher Robin."

Pooh, who had just put his paw into the tenth pot of honey, left it there, just to be on the safe side, and asked: "What about Christopher Robin?"

"The Rumour, Pooh. Do you suppose he has come back?"

Eeyore, the grey donkey, was standing at the edge of the Hundred Acre Wood, staring at a patch of thistles. He had been saving them for a Rainy Day and was beginning to wonder whether it would ever rain again and whether, by the time it did, there would be any juice left in them, when Pooh and Piglet came by.

"Hallo, little Piglet," said Eeyore. "Hallo, Pooh. And what are you doing around here?"

"We came to see you, Eeyore," said Pooh.

"A quiet day, was it, Pooh? An if-we-haven't-anything-better-to-do sort of day? How very thoughtful."

Piglet wondered how it was that every conversation with Eeyore seemed to go wrong.

"Time hanging heavy, was it, Piglet? And, Pooh, I would thank you not to stand on those thistles."

"Which ones would you like me to stand on?" asked Pooh.

"But, Eeyore," squeaked Piglet, "it's C–C–C–"

"Have you swallowed something, little Piglet? Not a thistle, I trust?"

"It's Christopher Robin," said Pooh. "He's coming back."

While Pooh was talking, Eeyore went rather still. Only his tail moved, brushing away an imaginary fly.

"Well," he said, rather huskily, then paused. "Well. Christopher Robin . . . That is to say . . . heretofore . . ." he blinked quickly several times. "Christopher Robin coming back. Well."

Finally, the Rumour was confirmed. Owl had flown to Rabbit's house, and Rabbit had spoken to his Friends and Relations, who had spoken to Smallest-of-All, who thought he had seen Christopher Robin but couldn't be absolutely certain because sometimes he remembered things which turned out not to have happened yet, or ever, or at all. And they asked Tigger what he thought, only he was hopping across Kanga's carpet avoiding the yellow bits, which could be dangerous, and paid no attention. But Kanga had told Rabbit that it was true, and when Kanga said something was true, then that thing *was* true. And so, if Pooh and Piglet thought that it was true, and Owl believed that it was true, and Kanga *said* that it was true, then it really must be true. Mustn't it?

So a meeting was convened to pass a Rissolution. The Rissolution was for a Welcum Back Party for Christopher Robin, and Roo got so excited that he fell into the brook once by accident, and twice on purpose, until Kanga told him that if he did it again he would not be allowed to come to the party, but would have to go home to bed.

* * *

It was July. The morning of the party dawned warm and sunny and the spinney in the Hundred Acre Wood was looking its finest. There were speckles of light on the ground where the sun had found a way through the branches, and other places where the branches had said No. Kanga found a mossy place and laid a table with her best linen tablecloth, the one with bunches of grapes embroidered around the edges, and Rabbit brought his best willow-pattern teacups, and said that they were Heirlooms, and when Pooh asked Owl in a whisper what an Heirloom was, Owl said that it was a kind of kite. Then Kanga moved one of the teacups so that it was covering the stain where Tigger had spilled a dollop of Roo's Strengthening Medicine.

All the animals brought treats for the feast: hazelnuts from the rabbits and a pot of honey (almost full) from Pooh, and a twist of lemon sherbet from Piglet, the kind that when you put it in the palm of your hand and licked it, the palm of your hand went bright yellow, and jellies of all colours made by Roo and Tigger. There were glasses with coloured straws and home-made lemonade, and squares of decorated paper with everybody's names on them, and things which you blew and which made a hooting noise when you did, and things which you threw, and balloons, long ones as well as round ones, and splendid crackers.

But in the very centre of the table stood the finest cake you ever saw, baked by Kanga and iced by Roo and Tigger, and there was spindly writing on the icing, except that nobody could make out what it said, not even Owl; and when Pooh asked Roo and Tigger what the writing said, they giggled and ran off to play in the bracken.

Everyone had been invited to the party, even Eeyore, and Pooh had pushed a special invitation under the door of Christopher Robin's house. Owl had written it. It said:

SPESHUL INVITATION
WELCUM HOME
CRHISTOPHER ROBIN
AND WELCUM TO A
WELCUM HOME PRATY
DAY: TODAY

"It says Welcum three times," Owl explained, "because that's how pleased we are to see him back."

All the animals sat on the ground and waited, but there was a tree stump reserved for Christopher Robin. The jellies were getting rather wobbly in the sun and Roo kept looking at the green jelly which he had made himself with grapes and greengages and which was – or at least had been – shaped like a castle. It was a little along the tablecloth from him and he kept fidgeting to get closer to it, because although he *thought* the others might like green best he *knew* that he did. He kept saying to anyone who would listen: "The red ones are the best. They've got strawberries in them. The yellow ones are even better, because they're really lemony." But he said nothing about the green ones.

Eeyore was the last of the animals to arrive in the spinney. He turned around a few times and sat down on the tree stump.

"Jollifications and hey-diddle-diddle," he said. "Decent of you to wait for me."

"But, Eeyore –" said Piglet, and would have said more if Kanga hadn't frowned and shaken her head at him.

"I'm sure it's going to be a lovely party," said Kanga, "but you're sitting in Christopher Robin's place, Eeyore dear."

Eeyore unfolded his legs and got slowly back to his feet. "It was quite comfortable," he said, "as tree stumps go. I'm sure Christopher Robin will enjoy sitting on it now that I've warmed it up for him."

Still there was no Christopher Robin.

Piglet held his cracker up to the light and shook it to see if it rattled. Then, a little sadly, he put it down again.

"When can we start? Oh, when can we start?" cried Baby Roo. "The red jellies are best everyone. Or the yellow ones. Oh, when can we start?"

And Kanga said: "Soon, dear, soon, but don't keep pointing like that. It's rude."

Pooh was staring at his pot of honey and getting drowsy, and wondering if it was still *his* pot of honey,

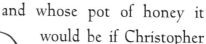

and whose pot of honey it would be if Christopher Robin didn't come, and whether one could train bees to make honey straight into pots, because then they could use the combs to brush their hair without it getting sticky. If bees have hair. And maybe he would leave an empty pot out there just in case. And would it get any hotter, and what would happen if it did . . . and Pooh's head sank forward and he uttered a soft sort of Snunt, which is halfway between a grunt and a snore.

Then, by way of conversation, Owl said: "Did I ever tell you about my Uncle Robert?" And although he had told them more than once, more than several times in fact, Kanga said quickly before he could begin: "Best not to tire ourselves. Christopher Robin is sure to be here soon." And Piglet said: "I expect he had to come a very long way."

"How do you know?" Rabbit asked. "How long?"

"He may have been delayed by a gorse bush," said Pooh. "They do that sometimes, you know."

"Or a Heffalump," said Piglet, and he shuddered at the thought.

Then the sun went behind the only cloud in the sky, and the speckles in the Forest went away and came back again, which is what Christopher Robin had done if you believed the Rumour.

Then Piglet, a little flustered and a little hungry, explained: "Christopher Robin has had to come from wherever he's coming from, Rabbit, and it must be a very

long way, because if it wasn't he would be here by now."

Just at that moment there was a whirring sound, and a clicketty sound, and a pinging sound, and there he was, Christopher Robin, just as he had always been, except that he was riding a bright blue bicycle. Everybody gasped and began chattering at the same time, which is usually quite impolite but wasn't just then. When Christopher Robin had leant his bicycle against a tree, he looked at them all and said: "Hallo, everyone, I'm back."

"Hallo," said Pooh, and Christopher Robin gave him a smile.

Owl said: "A velocipede. I will explain to you the principle upon which . . ."

Eeyore said: "A pleasure to see you, Christopher Robin, and I hope you enjoy the tree stump, which is quite warmed up."

Piglet just said: "Ooh!" He wanted to say much more, but the words wouldn't form themselves the way he wanted them to, and when they had, it was too late to use them.

Roo said: "There are lots of jellies, Christopher Robin, and me and Tigger made them, and the red ones have got real strawberries in them, but if you want a green one . . ."

"I'll try them all," said Christopher Robin cheerfully, "but I'll try the red ones first."

Early and Late, two smallish Friends and Relations, pulled a cracker, or tried to, and Early let go by mistake and Late toppled over backwards. But Winnie-the-Pooh

gave Christopher Robin a bear hug and said: "Welcome home, Christopher Robin."

Kanga said: "You must cut the cake, Christopher Robin."

"And make a wish," added Tigger, hopping from foot to foot, which is complicated when you have four.

So Christopher Robin made a wish, and everyone cheered and clapped and said: "Welcome home," except Eeyore who said: "Many happy returns of the day," and Christopher Robin felt glad to be back, but a little sad at the same time. Then everybody blew their hooters and threw their streamers and pulled their crackers, and Eeyore pulled two, one with his front hoofs and one with his back, and the first one had a motto and a key ring with A PRESENT FROM MARGATE on it and a paper hat, but the second only had a paper hat.

And Christopher Robin said to Pooh: "I've eaten a lot of jelly and two slices of Kanga's cake, so I don't have room for the honey.

I wondered, Pooh, whether you would be kind enough to eat it for me?" And Pooh was kind enough and did.

Then Eeyore said: "I don't suppose he remembers who I am. Not that it's important. After all why should he?"

*　　*　　*

When they had eaten everything they could eat, which was almost but not quite everything on the table, because at a proper tea party there should always be leftovers for the birds, Christopher Robin made this announcement.

"Now, dear friends of the Forest, in my bicycle basket I have Coming-Home Presents for you all, because I have missed you so much. And I have wrapped them up in Christmas paper because I had some left over from last year and I thought it might be useful for next year."

The animals were very excited, even Smallest-of-All, who had fallen asleep in a butter dish and had to be de-buttered. He thought that maybe it was Christmas already, so he opened his present, a shiny farthing with a wren on it, and said, "Happy Christmas, everybody!" Then he went straight back to sleep, because the moon was already shining out and it was that mysterious time between day and night when it is not easy to tell which is which or why or whether.

These were the presents Christopher Robin had brought for the other animals.

 For Early and Late: sugar mice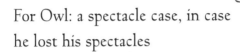

For Owl: a spectacle case, in case he lost his spectacles

 For Piglet: pink earmuffs

For Roo: a bottle of coloured sand in a satisfying pattern from the Isle of Wight

For Kanga: a set of seven thimbles (one for each day of the week)

For Tigger: a pogo stick

For Rabbit: a book called *1001 Useful Household Hints*

For Eeyore: two umbrellas, for front and back

 For Pooh: a wooden ladle for removing the sticky bits from pots of honey

What did Christopher Robin wish for when he cut the cake? That is a secret and if I told you what it was it would never come true, but Pooh came into it, and Piglet, and the sunshine, so it was quite a long wish and Christopher Robin kept his eyes tight shut when he made it, but his lips moved a bit.

If what Christopher Robin wished for was more adventures in the Hundred Acre Wood, then his wish certainly did come true and I will tell you about the adventures, from the time that Piglet Became a Hero to the time that Tigger Dreamt of Africa. There could well be Heffalumps in there somewhere, and honey. In fact, I am sure of the honey. There may even be a story about the bright blue bicycle, because it was a very fine one, a Raleigh, and it made you feel good just to look at it, and made you want to rub the mud off it just as soon as it got onto it. There might be other bicycles in the Hundred Acre Wood but none as fine nor as shiny as Christopher Robin's, and no boy prouder than he.

·CHAPTER TWO·

*in which Owl does a crossword,
and a Spelling Bee is held*

SINCE CHRISTOPHER ROBIN WENT AWAY Piglet had been staying at Pooh's house because Owl was staying at Piglet's, because – oh well, it would take too long to explain. A few days after Christopher Robin's return, Pooh and Piglet were sitting together over breakfast at that pleasant time of the day when you know that there is much to be done but not quite yet.

Pooh had completed his stoutness exercises – two push-ups, two pull-ups and a lie-down – and Piglet had written in his diary: *Got up. Had brekfast. Wrote this in diary,* and was wondering how he managed to Fit It All In, when Pooh said: "I wonder where Christopher Robin has been."

"I don't know," said Piglet, who had been wondering too. "But he's a bit grand, isn't he, Pooh, since he came back and he seems a bit more . . . a bit more . . ."

"That's it exactly," said Pooh, "a bit more but not too much . . ."

Piglet closed his diary.

"But he's still Christopher Robin."

"I wish I knew where he'd been," continued Pooh. "Do you think Owl would know?"

"He might do, Pooh, which would be good, and if he didn't he might make something up and that would be good too. Let's go and ask him."

On this particular morning, Owl had settled down

in his comfiest chair and folded the *Ornithological Times* so that the bit with the crossword puzzle was on top. On a low table next to him was a cup of tea, and he was wearing the old shawl that had belonged to Uncle Robert. It smelled a bit, but helped him to concentrate.

The first clue was 1 Across. It read: 'Big Bird (3 letters)'.

Owl scratched behind his ear with his quill pen. However, when he wrote down 'EGL' on a piece of scrap paper to see how it looked, it looked rather odd. When he held it up to the mirror, it looked even odder. But try as he might, he could not squeeze OSTRIDGE or even HORK into three letters.

"Bother!" muttered Owl, and stuck his quill through the newspaper.

At just that moment, Pooh and Piglet arrived at the front door and tugged at the handkerchief with a knot in it which served as a bell-pull.

Piglet cleared his throat. "We want to know, Owl, whether you know where Christopher Robin has been and whether he will be going there again, and when." The words came out in such a rush that Piglet blinked several times and steadied himself on the low table.

"He has been on Safari," said Owl impressively.

"What does that mean?" Pooh asked.

"It means that he has been so far and no farther. And now if you would be so kind as to close the door behind you when you leave."

"Why don't you come with us to Christopher Robin's house," said Piglet, "and we can ask him ourselves?"

"Oh, all right," said Owl, thinking that Christopher Robin would surely know what Big Bird (3 letters) would be.

It was a perfect summer day and the Forest was sparkling. The cobwebs on the bracken were strung with seed pearls of dew and the trees were competing as to which was wearing the brightest green. Christopher Robin was polishing his bicycle when the others arrived.

"Come indoors, Pooh and Piglet and Owl," said Christopher Robin, "because I have something to show you all and it is an Indoors Sort of Thing."

When Christopher Robin had finished wiping the polish off his fingers and onto his handkerchief and off his handkerchief and back onto his fingers, he handed Owl a very large book that was wrapped in tissue paper.

"I won this at school," he said, "for throwing the cricket ball more than fifty yards."

Pooh and Piglet glanced at each other. "You *were* at school!" cried Piglet in excitement. "I thought you were."

Meanwhile, Owl was unwrapping the book.

"It's a Thesaurus," said Christopher Robin.

"Is that like a Heffalump?" asked Piglet. "Oh dear. Oh dearie, dearie me."

"It's a book of words. You look up one word and it tells you lots of other words which mean the same thing."

"Why can't you just use the word you had in the first place?" asked Piglet.

"I don't know," said Christopher Robin. "Why don't we look something up and see?"

So Pooh looked up 'owl' and the book said: *sage, hooter, bird of ill omen.*

"Isn't *sage* a kind of herb?" asked Pooh.

"It means someone who's wise," said Christopher Robin.

"Indeed," said Owl, fluffing out his feathers, and then he thought for a while, and said: "Indeed" again and "Indeed . . . hmm," and saying indeed three times made it seem as though Owl was having a sage and wise and hooterish kind of thought. "The animals around here are not well educated, Christopher Robin, not like you and I."

"You and me," said Christopher Robin.

"Yes," said Owl, "both of us. Just so. I expect the Thesaurus would help me with my crossword puzzle. I don't suppose you could have a look at 1 Across?"

"Crossword puzzles," cried Christopher Robin in delight. "We were doing them at school."

"What else did you do at school, Christopher Robin?" asked Pooh. "And did you have elevenses there?"

"Well, let me see now," said Christopher Robin, for to tell the truth school already seemed a long time ago. "It was noisy and the geography teacher only had one eye and it smelled a bit of floor polish – the school, I mean, not the eye. There was maths and cricket and a Spelling Bee."

"A bee?" asked Pooh.

"We could have a Spelling Bee here," Christopher Robin suggested, "if you would like to. And you, Owl, could be the quizmaster."

"Good idea," said Owl. "It's not the animals' fault that they are ignorant."

*   *   *

That night as they lay in bed, Piglet asked Pooh about the Thesaurus.

"It's just a big book, Piglet."

"It's not a great big monster?"

"No, Piglet."

"Not at all like a Heffalump?"

"Go to sleep, Piglet."

"And the words aren't very cross, are they, Pooh?" added Piglet, shivering a little. "I wonder, can we leave the light on tonight?"

The next day, which was the day of the Grand Spelling Bee, the sky was stormy with white clouds like marshmallow scudding across it. Near the horizon there were some darker ones which looked as if they Meant Business.

In the clearing there was a placard slung between two larch trees. Owl had made it. It read:

GRAND SPELLING BEE
ALL WELCUM

A few logs had been placed end to end for sitting on, with larger ones in front for writing on. Pencils had been sharpened and squares of paper laid ready with the name of each animal proudly displayed in BLOCK CAPITALS. Owl was wearing his pince-nez glasses, which he kept on a chain around his neck, and a tweed waistcoat which had belonged to his Uncle Robert, who had been a Credit to the Family Despite Everything.

Rabbit and Kanga and Roo were there, and Tigger and Piglet, and Early and Late and Friends and Relations (not all of them, but quite enough to be going on with) and Henry Rush, the beetle.

It looked like it might rain.

"Is everybody ready?" asked Owl, taking a gold watch out of his waistcoat pocket and putting it to his ear. The watch had stopped many years ago at 3.15, which was a good time to have stopped at.

One of the Friends and Relations sniffed loudly.

"Use your handkerchief," said Rabbit.

"Haven't got one," sulked the young relation, and sniffed again. "Haven't got a name either."

"You must have a name," said Rabbit. "Everybody's got a name. I expect it's Jack."

Owl cleared his throat loudly and said again: "Is everybody ready?"

Piglet was wondering if they could have a competition for drawing instead of spelling. He could draw a table

so that you could see all four legs at once and that's really difficult. And a vase of flowers on top.

Pooh said to Piglet: "It's all right, Piglet. Spelling is easy once you get started."

Piglet nodded. "Getting started is the worst bit. I expect we'll start soon."

Tigger had drawn a noughts-and-crosses at the top of his piece of paper and he and Roo were playing, but since both of them wanted to be crosses, the game was turning out rather noisy and confused.

"I've won," cried Tigger and Roo at the same moment.

There was a dusty smell in the air, and a few heavy spots of rain plopped onto the sheets of paper. A rumble of thunder echoed around the spinney, as if the storm was considering the possibilities.

In the sky, a flock of starlings that had been flying west changed their minds all at the same time and veered off to the south-east. Lightning flickered above the larches and another rumble of thunder stopped being side-drums and became cymbals.

"Ooh," said Piglet, "why is it doing that and I wish it wouldn't!"

Owl adjusted his pince-nez and glared at the animals so fiercely that one of the youngest hid under a toadstool. "Ready or not," Owl said, "the first word is Fiddlesticks."

There were groans on all sides.

"Can *you* spell it, Owl?" asked Rabbit, and the cry was taken up by most of the other animals.

"Of course I can," said Owl.

"Then do it," said Rabbit.

"Shan't," said Owl. "The second word is Rhododendron."

"I thought there were going to be bees," said Pooh, and Piglet said: "I thought so too, and I don't think anybody in the world can spell Rhodothingamajig."

"And why would they want to?" added Pooh.

"And the third word is –"

But the third word wasn't because just then a large drop of rain landed on the dictionary and an even larger one landed on Owl's spectacles. Within seconds the Forest was asparkle with raindrops coming down and raindrops bouncing back up.

Christopher Robin jumped onto the tree stump and made an announcement.

"Friends, the Spelling Bee has been cancelled, because spelling is difficult enough at the best of times, and impossible in the rain." At this the animals cheered loudly. "But why don't you all come back to my house and we'll toast some muffins and make a huge house of cards."

"But Christopher Robin –" objected Owl.

"It's all right, Owl. When a Spelling Bee is interrupted by the weather the prize goes to the quizmaster, which is you."

Owl took off his pince-nez, blinked a few times, then wiped the lenses, and asked: "Me?"

"Yes, Owl, you."

With which Christopher Robin handed over the prize, which turned out to be a crossword puzzle book with all the answers at the end. Owl was very proud, and also suddenly a little thoughtful.

Then Christopher Robin led the animals back to his house. There they had muffins toasted to perfection, and Kanga spread yellow butter on them so that it melted into the crevices. For those who wanted it – which was everybody – there was jam with whole strawberries in it to go on top.

When they had eaten all the muffins and drunk cups of tea from china cups with roses around the sides, a pleased-looking Owl went up to Christopher Robin.

"Big Bird in three letters," he said.

"Yes?"

"It's *owl*, of course!"

"Why so it is!" Christopher Robin agreed.

After that, the animals settled down and made the biggest house of cards ever seen in the Hundred Acre Wood, with turrets and bridges and a yard for the carriages. When there were no cards left, Tigger bounced onto the middle of it so that it collapsed quite flat, but nobody minded because by then the storm had passed and the evening sun was peering anxiously over the rim of the hill. The moon was there too, so that everybody knew that it was time to go home to bed.

Pooh stayed at Christopher Robin's house that night and watched him have his bath. What he really wanted to see was whether he still wore his blue braces, and, yes, he did (but not in the bath).

·CHAPTER THREE·

in which Rabbit organises almost everything

RABBIT WAS THE MOST SENSIBLE of animals. If you were to ask anyone in the Hundred Acre Wood, "Is there anybody sensible around here?" they would be sure to say: "Go and see Rabbit."

When you arrived at Rabbit's house, which was a hole in the ground with a front door and a back door – very sensible – Rabbit would ask who you were and, if you were who Rabbit thought you ought to be, you would be invited in.

Rabbit's front room had sensible things in it like calendars and colanders and fireside rugs, and fire irons and sturdy Royal Doulton china, and a map of Bournemouth on the wall. Once you were seated, Rabbit would bring you a sensible cup of tea on a large saucer in case of drips and, by way of a treat, a small piece of shortbread from a tin with a picture of Edinburgh Castle on the top. Then, having made sure that you didn't scatter any crumbs, he would send you back where you'd come from.

"It's just as well there's somebody around these parts who has some sense," Rabbit used to say on these occasions, "otherwise anything might happen."

If someone asked Rabbit what that anything might be, he would reply: "Pirates, revolution, things thrown on the ground and not picked up. And you should always carry a clean handkerchief with you just in case."

One day, when Rabbit and Christopher Robin and Pooh were having tea on a sunny bank not far from Rabbit's house, they found the conversation going just this way. They'd got to the bit about revolution, at which point Pooh stuck his head right into his pot of honey.

"Which reminds me," continued Rabbit regardless, "nobody eats sensibly around here. Everyone should have allotments like mine. Then we could grow vegetables in rows like the Romans did."

"Did the Romans grow vegetables in rows?" asked Christopher Robin.

"Well," Rabbit replied, "if they had grown vegetables they would have been in rows, because it's too difficult to grow things in circles."

Then, leaning in close to Pooh, he said: "Consider all that honey and condensed milk. It cannot be good for you. You should eat as I do."

Pooh pulled his head out of the honey pot, and stared at Rabbit.

"I propose rationing you to one pot a month and replacing the honey with home-grown carrots and radishes."

"Radishes!" Pooh cried in dismay.

"Just joking," said Rabbit. But if Rabbit was only teasing Pooh about his honey, he was serious about organising things in the Forest.

"What we most need around here," he announced, "apart from allotments and sensible diets and some overdue hedging and ditching, is a Census."

Pooh licked the honey from his nose and asked Rabbit what he meant.

"A Census is when you write down the names of everyone who is living in a place, and how many of them, and so on."

"But why, Rabbit?"

"So that if anyone wants to know you can tell them straightaway. The Ancient Britons did it in the Domesday Book, and once they knew who there was and where they were . . ." Rabbit paused to catch up with himself, "they could tax them."

"Why did they want to?" Christopher Robin asked, reasonably enough.

"To pay for the Census, of course," answered Rabbit. "I thought everybody knew that."

As word got about, the other animals expressed their doubts.

"It seems to me," Kanga remarked, "that you can't count *everything*."

Piglet said: "It's not a Census, it's a Nonsensus," and then blushed at his cleverness.

Having announced to the world that a Census was what the Forest needed, Rabbit had no choice but to organise one. His first port of call was Owl's house. He pulled on the bell-pull, then went in without waiting for an answer.

Owl was toying with a metal puzzle that he had found in his Christmas cracker three years ago, along with a paper hat and a joke about giraffes.

"What is it now, Rabbit?" he complained.

"I have to ask you questions for the Census."

"Very well. But be quick about it."

"Name?"

"Owl."

"Spell it."

"W-O-L."

"Age?"

"Mind your own business!"

"Occupation?"

"Enough, Rabbit, enough!"

Owl flapped his wings so crossly that Rabbit flattened his ears and scuttled out of the house.

His next destination was Eeyore's Gloomy Place where the old grey donkey was standing in the sun, dreaming of being young again in a field of poppies.

"Go away, Rabbit," he muttered, opening an eye. "I was happy."

"Happy may be all very well, Eeyore, but it doesn't butter any parsnips."

"Then leave them unbuttered," said Eeyore, and he put his head

between his legs, which is the second rudest thing a donkey can do.

"Well, really," said Rabbit, "some animals!"

But Eeyore had shut his eyes and was trying to get back into the dream.

Next on Rabbit's list was Christopher Robin, whom he found sketching the Six Pine Trees.

"Hallo, Rabbit. How's the Census going?"

"Very well, very well, if we exclude certain donkeys. After all, a thing begun is a thing half done."

Christopher Robin frowned over his sketch.

"I don't think so, Rabbit. If I begin to read a book that has a hundred pages, I begin on page one but it isn't half done until I get to page fifty, agreed?"

But Rabbit was not really listening.

"Name?" he asked.

"You know my name, Rabbit," said Christopher Robin.

"Spell it."

"I-T," said Christopher Robin.

Then he looked back at his sketch and added a bit of shadow where a shadow ought to be: "Oh, Rabbit, I have better things to do."

Rabbit went away muttering. It might have been something about No Sense of Social Responsibility, but then again it might not.

At Kanga's house, Roo and Tigger were playing a game called Licking the Mixing Bowl Clean. It was a game without rules except that the winner was the one who finished last.

"Tigger," said Rabbit, "let's begin with you."

"Yes, let's," said Tigger bouncing a little, even though he had no idea what was to be begun. He liked to be asked to do things, and he liked to be asked to do them first, and he always said 'yes' because it is much more interesting when you do.

"Name?"

"Tigger."

"Spell it."

"T-I-GRRRRRRRRR . . ." And Tigger emitted a ferocious growl.

"Put your handkerchief in front of your mouth when you do that, dear," said Kanga.

"Age?"

Tigger counted his paws, and then his whiskers, and then Roo's paws and whiskers, and then Kanga's paws and whiskers.

"Don't know," he said at last.

"I'll put down twelve," said Rabbit.

"Hooray!" cried Tigger. "Then I can have a birthday."

When Rabbit had put all the information from the Census together, he created a chart. He coloured it using a set of crayons that were still in their matching paper wrappers, and then took it along to show Christopher Robin.

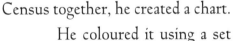

"Very fine, Rabbit," said Christopher Robin, "but why aren't *you* on the chart?"

Rabbit stared at the paper.

"Ah," he said eventually, shuffling his feet. "It was . . ." he continued, looking at the floor, "an Oversight."

"Then you'd better complete the job."

Rabbit found that answering his own questions was simple enough to start with. How old was he? Five seemed about right. What was his occupation? Rabbit thought for a bit, then wrote 'Importent Things'.

Before long, he got to the question about the size of his family. Wherever Rabbit turned there were Friends and Relations. There always had been. But which were Friends and which were Relations?

Once upon a time he had bought a special diary and tried to jot down all their birthdays, but even for a sensible and organised animal like Rabbit it was more than he could cope with.

So he went to see Grandad Buck, who was Very Ancient and the Head of the Rabbit Family.

Grandad Buck did not entirely approve of Rabbit, partly because he did not entirely approve of anyone, but he listened intently, thought for a few moments, and then said, rather grandly: "My advice to you is to spread the word that all your Friends and Relations are invited to your abode. Promise them food. Then, as they arrive, get their names and ages. That should do the trick."

He paused, then looked hard at Rabbit, and barked: "Now, young fellow, I must ask you please to go away."

Rabbit did just as Grandad Buck had advised, promising carrots for Relations and shortbread for Friends. And in due course, on the day selected, Rabbit opened the door at 8.30 am sharp and the first rabbit demanded her shortbread.

"But you're a relation," objected Rabbit. "You get carrots."

The little rabbit put her paws over her floppy ears.

"Am not a Relation! I want shortbread!"

So as not to hold things up, Rabbit gave her a piece. Within an hour he had taken down the details of three hedgehogs, four mice, six squirrels, three beetles, and also twenty-one rabbits – all of whom claimed to be 'Friends'. The shortbread from the tin with the picture of Edinburgh Castle on the lid was long gone, and the home-made jam was going the same way. Rabbit was running out of paper, and still the queue stretched all the way to Kanga's house.

Many of the younger ones discovered the Sandy Pit in which Roo played, and approved of it and played in it themselves.

The carrots from Rabbit's allotment lay neglected. Friends who had come too late for shortbread became very cross and started rampaging around the place, until Rabbit's sensible and tidy drawing room was thrown into disarray and covered in muddy and sandy paw-prints everywhere. Some of the younger element invented a game which involved rolling yourself up in the fireside rug with a lace doily on your head and

 pretending to be Sultans and Sultanas. The beautiful chart was drawn on with the crayons, which had all been taken out of their tins.

The Royal Doulton china was knocked over, and as for the beautiful allotment where Rabbit had grown his carrots, it was in severe danger.

"Behave yourselves!" Rabbit cried. "Set an example. Be sensible!"

"But we are your guests and you promised us shortbread," said the rabbits, "and you haven't got any, so phooey to you with knobs on!"

"Then eat these lovely carrots and behave!" retorted Rabbit shrilly.

But the little rabbits said they were bored with carrots and began to sing: "Why are we waiting?"

"Go on waiting!" shouted Rabbit, who was by now in a Real State.

He rushed out of his house and all the way to Pooh's house without stopping once. When he'd arrived and gathered his breath sufficiently, he explained what had happened . . . and then the world seemed to slow down a little as Pooh said comforting things like "There, there, Rabbit," and "Never mind, it's all over now," (which it probably wasn't, but that is the kind of thing you should say to a once-sensible Rabbit in distress).

"How about some cocoa and a little smackerel of something?" Pooh suggested. Then, after thinking for a moment he changed this to, "Or just some cocoa, and I'll eat the something for you, so you won't be unhealthy?"

But Rabbit seemed very keen on having a smackerel of

something too. After eating all the honey and condensed milk that Pooh reluctantly set before him, he sat back with his paws wrapped around the mug of cocoa.

"I thought I was a sensible animal," Rabbit said, shuddering.

"Of course you are," said Pooh, "everybody knows that."

"And it was such a sensible idea, the Census."

"It's almost the same word," agreed Pooh.

"And the allotments, Pooh. Vegetables for everyone."

"And honey for some," said Pooh seriously, licking a smear of yellow from the edge of his plate.

Rabbit felt that Pooh had perhaps missed something here, but it seemed too complicated to argue. Instead, he said goodnight to a surprised Piglet, who had just come in from rolling in the dirt and was a friendly brown

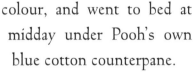

colour, and went to bed at midday under Pooh's own blue cotton counterpane.

When the evening came, Rabbit slept on, but Pooh didn't mind. He took an old blanket and bedded down by his honey cupboard, to reassure the pots that they would be safe.

In the morning, some slightly sheepish-looking Friends and Relations came knocking on the door. They asked Pooh if he knew where Rabbit was.

"He's aslee –" Pooh started, then he thought for a bit. He thought of Rabbit, and what Rabbit would say if he were here, and if he were himself again.

"My dear friend Rabbit . . ." started Pooh as importantly as he could. "My *very* dear friend Rabbit told me to tell you that the job for today is to tidy everything in his house and make it as organdised as possible. Things in rows . . . and . . . and things. Rabbit will supervise us, in case we put stuff back in the wrong places."

So they all went over to Rabbit's house, and it took less time than anyone expected to get the place shining clean. While they cleaned and dusted and polished, they each sang their favourite songs, and Piglet sang one he had learned in French from Christopher Robin, about a man called Frère Jacques who spent his

time ringing bells. Then, because it was voted the best, he sang it again with all of them joining in the chorus – even Rabbit. Although Owl muttered, "He's a little off-key." But nobody noticed or knew what he meant.

·CHAPTER FOUR·

*in which it stops raining for ever,
and something slinky comes out of the river*

NOBODY COULD REMEMBER ANYTHING like it. It had not rained for forty days and forty nights, and it kept getting hotter. Little streams high up in the Forest became lazy and lost their sparkle. The boggy bit near Eeyore's Gloomy Place stopped being boggy, and the big river became no more than a trickle, so that Roo could hop across it, jumping from stone to stone, without getting his tail wet.

Then it got even hotter. In his thick coat, Tigger hardly bounced at all, while Piglet would go to lie in Eeyore's shadow and Eeyore would swish his tail to keep the flies away.

Still Owl's barometer said Set Fair, and, when he tapped it, it still said Set Fair, and when he tapped it again it fell onto the floor and the glass broke, but it still said Set Fair and still there was no rain.

The river got thinner and thinner until it was little more than a few paddling pools which Roo went paddling in when Kanga wasn't looking and sometimes when she was, and, when he came in for tea, he left little paw-shaped patches on the carpet. At the bottom of a dried-out hollow, Eeyore found an old tin trunk with *HMS Fortitude* on the side, and he thought that if it ever did rain again, this would be a good place to store the water.

Christopher Robin and Pooh helped Eeyore to drag the trunk out of the hollow, then sat on the grass to rest.

Pooh said to Christopher Robin:
"It's all very well for you,
Christopher Robin, because
you can take your things off,
but I can't take my fur off."

But Christopher Robin
was too hot to reply.

Then one day, which some said was the hottest yet and others said was the hottest ever, something long and slinky and furry and whiskery came out of what had once been a river but now was little better than a mud patch.

"Oh, la!" said the Silver-and-Silky Slinky Thing, sitting up straight as a beech tree and looking around with beady eyes. "What is a self-respecting otter to do when she can't have a bath? And," she added in a haughty voice, "when she has nothing to eat?"

"Are you talking to me?" asked Rabbit, who was bringing what was left of his washing to what was left of the stream.

"And who are you, Long Ears?"

"I am Rabbit," said Rabbit, startled and rather offended. "And who are you?"

"I am asking the questions, Bunny Rabbit. Unless you are cleverer than I am, which I don't suppose you are, looking as if you have just been dragged out of a conjuror's hat."

Rabbit was so worried at being spoken to like this that he didn't know which way to look. When the Slinky Thing saw this she grunted a few times, which was as close as she could come to a chuckle.

"Well, Bunny, if you must know, my name is Lottie. But you haven't answered my questions."

"What were they again?"

"I can't remember," said Lottie.

"I'll go and ask Christopher Robin," said Rabbit, and he scuttled away a little faster than usual.

Christopher Robin was looking at an atlas. "I wonder why so many of the countries are pink?" he said.

"I haven't time for all that now," said Rabbit.

"Well, if you were to visit them, the ground wouldn't be pink, would it? And if the world is round why is the atlas flat?"

"Oh dear," said Rabbit beginning to panic because of so many questions in a single morning. Not knowing the answers, he changed the subject. "Anyway, Christopher Robin, something has just come out of the river and it wants a bath and something to eat. I think it's an otter."

"I've got a bath," said Christopher Robin cheerfully. "And there's some potted meat in the larder. Do you think that would do?"

"Perhaps you should come and ask her yourself."

By the time they got to the oozy bit that had once been a proper stream, quite a few of the animals had gathered around the otter, who was twisting and turning in front of them like a ballerina in a musical box.

"My name is Lottie," she announced. "See my fine fur coat, which is the colour of silver when the sun shines upon it, and pewter when it's cloudy. And see," she added, "my golden eyes, and my long tail which I call my rudder. It has been much admired for its length and flexibility. And beware," she concluded, "my red tongue and my white teeth, which are sharp enough, I can promise you, when they need to be."

Then, just when the animals were becoming alarmed, she rolled over a few times and slithered off to hide in the bushes.

"Catch me if you can," she cried. "Bet you can't!"

For a while the animals tried their hardest *not* to find Lottie, which was difficult because her tail was sticking out a good six inches. But then Tigger accidentally stepped on it and Lottie made a growling noise, so the game was up.

"Welcome to the Forest," said Christopher Robin quickly, before anything more disturbing could happen. "I'm Christopher Robin, and you're welcome to have a bath at my house, if that's what you would like."

Lottie reappeared from behind the bushes and bobbed her head gracefully.

"Thank you so much, Mr Robin. I would not trouble you if I were not in great need."

Then they all made their way to Christopher Robin's house, where Christopher Robin ran a bath and helped Lottie to climb in.

"Colder, Mr Robin," she said. "I like it nice and cold; it keeps me alert."

She swam around for a while, tossing the sponge into the air and catching it, and curling herself into a tight ball and spinning around with grunts of satisfaction and delight. But when Christopher Robin offered her potted meat, Lottie said: "Eels and frogs are what otters eat, so that is what I shall expect for my supper."

"I don't think we have any eels or frogs, Lottie, but would sardines do?"

"Are they Portuguese?"

"I expect some of them are."

"Are they in olive oil or tomato sauce?"

"Gosh!" said Christopher Robin who was not used to being quizzed like this, not even at school, and he went to the larder and came back with a tin.

"In the best houses," said Lottie, "they serve both kinds and have pilchards in the servants' quarters!"

Christopher Robin wrapped Lottie in a yellow towel and carried her into the sitting room. He brought her sardines in olive oil on a blue dish, and she ate them hungrily, chewing up the crunchy bits and commenting: "Not bad."

"And now," she said, "I shall play you a tune on my mouth organ." She did it very prettily, so that the animals clapped and the bolder ones shouted, "Bravo, Lottie."

"Thank you. I believe I shall stay," she told them, curtseying.

*   *   *

And still it did not rain. Eeyore tried to lie down in his shadow, but no matter how he tried it was always too quick for him, and when that did not work he licked the dew off the blackberry brambles.

"It's not much fun," he said, "especially when there are cobwebs on them, which there usually are in the mornings, but it's better than nothing."

One day, when Christopher Robin turned on the taps to run Lottie's bath, there was a sort of coughing noise and all that emerged from the pipe was a trickle of brownish water and a deep sigh.

"Oh, la!" cried Lottie. "I'm not getting into that. I still have standards!"

There was nothing for it but to call a Meeting. Owl drew up the Agenda, which read:

1. Minnits of the last meeting

2. Lak of water

3. Any other bizness

It was Owl who called the meeting to order.

"Item one," he said. "Minutes of the last meeting."

"There aren't any," said Christopher Robin, "because there wasn't one. And even if there had been, there wouldn't have been."

The animals murmured their approval.

"Very well," said Owl a bit grudgingly, "that's passed. Item two."

"It seems to me," said Rabbit, "that we need water and we don't have any. Which means that we need to get some."

"And quickly!" Lottie added.

"This is true," admitted Owl. "But where will we get some from?"

Eeyore raised a hoof. "If anyone's interested in hearing what I have to say, which I don't suppose they are, but I'll say it anyway . . . Where was I? Oh, yes, if people in this Forest thought a bit more, instead of just minuting all the time, they might remember that there used to be an old well near Galleon's Lap. At least, I think there did."

"But is it still there?" asked Rabbit. "And can we find it and will there be water in it if it is and if we can?"

"Possibly Not and Possibly Not and Possibly Not," said Eeyore, "and three Possiblys add up to one Probably."

"Then we must go in search of it," said Owl.

They might not have found the old well had it not been for Lottie. As they approached the clump of ivy

and gorse which concealed the opening, she suddenly sat up, the hair on her back bristling, her head high, her ears laid back, her nose twitching. Very softly she said: "It is here. I can scent it. Water is to an otter as air is to a bird."

With that, the animals set about clearing away the smaller plants while Christopher Robin hacked at the big ones. Soon a hole in the ground appeared right in front of them.

Around the hole, which Christopher Robin called a shaft, was a circle of rotten wood crawling with wood lice, an old rusted bucket on a rickety-looking chain, and an even rustier winch.

Piglet stared nervously over the edge. "It goes down and down," he said.

"It seems to me," said Christopher Robin sensibly, "that now we know that there's a well here, we need to make sure that there's water in it, and the way to do that is to throw something down and listen for a splash. Does anyone have a pebble?"

"I have," said Tigger, "but it's a very special one that I was keeping for my Collection of Special and Interesting Stones."

"Tigger," said Rabbit severely,

"what we have to consider here is the Greater Good of the Greater Number. Give me your pebble."

"Must I?" But even as Tigger asked, he knew what the answer would be.

Then Rabbit took Tigger's pebble and held it high above the shaft and called for silence and let it drop. The animals listened for what seemed like several minutes but was probably just a few seconds, and then unmistakably there could be heard a faint splash.

"Well," said Christopher Robin, "that is very good news indeed."

"It is good news, I quite see that, Christopher Robin," said Pooh, "but if the water is down there and we are up here . . ."

"The answer is the bucket," said Christopher Robin. "We let down the bucket, and it gets filled with water, and then we pull it up."

This suggestion met with general approval, and Pooh said: "What it is to have a Brain!"

And Christopher Robin said: "Silly old Pooh!" and dropped the bucket down the well. They all watched as the chain unwound and the winch spun with a racket like a hundred saucepans being thrown onto a tin roof, until suddenly everything stopped. The bucket stopped and the winch stopped and the noise stopped.

"Machinery!" muttered Eeyore. "Modern inventions! Never as good as they're cracked up to be."

"There must be a blockage," said Christopher Robin. "The pebble missed it but the bucket didn't. What we need is . . ." and then he stopped and glanced around the animals, and cleared his throat, and continued: "What we need is a Brave Volunteer to go down in the bucket to Clear the Obstruction and come back up with some water."

There was a long silence in Galleon's Lap, broken only by the wind in the pine trees and a distant buzzing of bees.

"Of course it has to be somebody who is not only brave but small."

There was another long silence. When Piglet looked at the other animals, he noticed that they were all staring at him.

"Oh dear," he squeaked. "Why is everyone looking at me?" But he already knew why. "Oh dear," he repeated, "oh dearie me."

So then he climbed into the bucket, and stood with his face just peeping over the edge.

"I don't much want to be here," he said.

Eeyore took hold of the winch:
"If you want me to pull you up, little Piglet, just shout 'Up!' and if you want to go deeper –"

"Deeper?" squeaked Piglet.

"– just shout 'Deeper!'"

"Oh," squeaked Piglet again. "Oh dearie, dearie me."

"Winch away!" cried Christopher Robin, and away Eeyore winched. The wood creaked and the chain rattled and ever so slowly the bucket vanished from sight.

Piglet, peering over the top of the bucket, could see the faces of his friends growing smaller and smaller. He could not quite smother a squeak of alarm, which echoed around him. The rope swayed, and it grew ever darker, and Piglet clutched the edge of the bucket with all his might.

"What if the chain breaks?" he whispered to himself. "And what if the bucket falls to bits, and what if the blockage is a Woozle, or Several Woozles, and what if they forget that I'm down here and go home and have tea and toasted buns?"

All around him came ghostly echoes whispering 'toasted buns, toasted buns' and Piglet kept trying to think of a hum to cheer himself up, but he couldn't.

Then suddenly the bucket stopped.

Piglet could just make out the blockage. It was a holly branch that was jammed in the wall.

Piglet grabbed hold of it, and shook it as hard as he dared. It fell right away, and there was a splash, and the bucket went down very fast after the tree branch – until there was another splash, and Piglet found himself bobbing around on an ocean of dark, glittering water.

Now he knew what had to be done.

1. He tilted the bucket and pushed it under the water until it was half full and he was three-quarters wet. Then,

2. He stood on the rim of the bucket and held very tight onto the chain. And then,

3. He shouted at the very top of his little voice: "Up! Up! Up, Eeyore, UP!"

He heard his voice echoing all around. After a while, the bucket began to rise and Piglet, balancing carefully on the rim and clutching the chain, went with it. The circle of light at the top of the shaft grew larger and lighter, and there were all the faces of his friends smiling down. Soon he could feel the sun on his face and see good old Eeyore turning the winch. He could hear the cheers and hoorays ringing out, and they were all for him, for Piglet.

He said in his proudest voice to all his friends: "It was nothing," but in his heart he knew that it was not nothing but Something Very Big Indeed.

For the next few days, while the Friends and Relations dug a ditch running downhill from the well to Eeyore's Gloomy Place, enough water was collected to run down the ditch and fill Eeyore's tin trunk to the brim. There Lottie made her home, which she called Fortitude Hall.

A new game became popular in the Forest. It was called Doing the Ditch, and, when the rains came, which in due course they did, as they always will, the nimbler animals would run up to Galleon's Lap and throw themselves into the ditch and be washed all the way down the hill to Eeyore's Place. Lottie was the quickest at it because her skin was the sleekest, and she would add little twists and turns along the way.

"Oh, la la!" she would cry as she landed in a heap at the bottom. And then she would play a twiddly bit on her mouth organ because she was having such fun.

Late one evening, a few days after this big adventure, when Piglet was thinking of going to bed, and thinking how nice it would be if he were already in bed, and what a bore it was that he wasn't already in bed, and how he liked his yellow pyjamas much better than his green ones, there was a knock on the door. It was Pooh.

"Sorry to come home so late, Piglet, but it takes time, you know."

"What does, Pooh?"

"Hums does. You think one is coming and it really wants to come only it suddenly decides that it won't come until later, and maybe not even then.

Like sneezing. And then, Piglet, it comes all of a sudden and you have to be ready for it with a piece of paper."

"The sneeze?"

"The hum."

"Oh, Pooh!" cried Piglet. "Is it a very long one?"

"Longer than most and almost as long as some," said Pooh.

Then Piglet got into his best listening position, which he did by burrowing down in the cushion that lay on the chair with the lilac upholstery. He felt himself getting rather red in the face, especially when Pooh cleared his throat and began.

Oh, it wouldn't rain and it wouldn't snow
And the sun shone all day long – ho!

At this point, Pooh broke off.

"You must join in with the 'Ho's when you get to know when they are coming, Piglet," he said.

"I will, Pooh. Ho! Is that right?"

"It's just right," said Pooh, and he went on:

Oh, it wouldn't rain and it wouldn't snow
And the sun shone all day long – ho!
And there wasn't a cloud in the whole of the sky
And the river ran wet until it ran dry
And all of the animals standing by
Cried ho, ho, ho!

"Ho!" said Piglet, and smiled happily.

Oh, it wouldn't rain and it wouldn't snow
And the sun shone all day long – ho!
Then out of the river there came a – what?
A thing called – what was it called? – an ott
Whose name was Lottie, unless it was not
With a ho, ho, diddle-dum, ho!

"Ho!" said Piglet, but this time he sounded a little worried.

Oh, it didn't rain and it wouldn't snow
And the sun shone all day long – ho!
Then Eeyore remembered there once was a well
But where it had been he could no longer tell
But Lottie could smell it – a watery smell,
With a diddle-dum, diddle-dum, ho!

"Ho," said Piglet in a rather quiet voice.

Oh, it hasn't rained and it hasn't snowed
And the sun shines all day long – ho!
But there's water now in our friendly wood,
Which when it is hot feels extremely good,
And if you don't join in this song you should!
With a ho, ho, diddle-dum, ho,
With a ho, ho, ho, ho . . .

"Ho," whispered Piglet in the tiniest voice yet.

"What's wrong, Piglet?" asked Pooh anxiously. "Don't you like my new hum?"

"Yes, Pooh," said Piglet, "I do rather like it. And all the ho, ho, hos and everything. But . . . but . . ."

"Anyway, Piglet, I must go to bed now that you've heard the hum, and I was so pleased that you were the first to hear it. Tomorrow we'll go and hum it to the others," said Pooh, and he went off happily to bed.

But long after Pooh was asleep, Piglet lay awake thinking about hums, and why this one had seemed a little . . . a little . . .

"I mean the arrival of an otter in the Forest," (he said to himself with a frown of concentration), "is certainly a big thing. And finding water when you need it is a very big thing. And nobody in the world heard Pooh's hum before I did, and tomorrow we're going to hum it to the others together, and that's something too, so if the hum was a little . . . not quite . . . well, it doesn't really matter. Maybe tomorrow there will be another adventure with me in it, and Pooh will write another hum about it, and then I shan't feel quite so . . . quite so . . ."

But before he knew exactly what he might not feel quite so-ish about, he had fallen asleep and was dreaming about a tame Heffalump and a friendly Thesaurus, and snoring a few very quiet snores, although of course there was nobody there to hear him, so you and I are the only ones to know.

·CHAPTER FIVE·

in which Pooh goes in search of honey

ONE MORNING WHEN Winnie-the-Pooh was Doing Nothing Very Much, but doing it rather well, he thought he would call on his old friend Christopher Robin and see whether he was doing anything. If not, perhaps they could do nothing together, because there are few things nicer than doing nothing with a friend.

"Are you busy?" enquired Pooh.

"As busy as a bee," said Christopher Robin, "which is not really very busy at all since all bees seem to do is buzz."

"And make honey, don't forget that. And speaking of honey . . ."

"My goodness, it's nearly time for elevenses," said Christopher Robin as Pooh sat down. "Would you care for some toast and marmalade?"

"I do believe I would," said Pooh gravely. "I don't suppose you could see your way . . ."

"'Fraid not," said Christopher Robin, "right out of honey. But there's some condensed milk."

So they both had a slice of toast and marmalade, cut into strips which Christopher Robin called 'soldiers'. Then, while they ate, Pooh asked a difficult question.

"I have been thinking about honey," he said, "and how we get it from the bees. Do you think they mind us taking it?"

"They probably want us to," said Christopher Robin, "otherwise they'd run out of room. Like cows and milk."

Pooh said: "I think we ought to say thank you to them."

"That's an excellent idea. Shall we go now? There's No Time Like the Present."

Pooh wrinkled his brow. "But we don't have a present, do we? I wonder what the bees would like."

Christopher Robin thought for a while, then decided

to take them a model aeroplane, "Because they must be interested in flying." Also a Yo-Yo because he had two, and a tin model of a farmhouse complete with climbing roses.

"If I were a bee," said Pooh, "I would like best something beginning with B, but the only thing I can think of beginning with B is 'bee' and they've got plenty of those already."

"How about bread-and-butter?" suggested Christopher Robin.

So it was agreed that along with the aeroplane and the Yo-Yo and the farmhouse, they would take bread-and-butter wrapped up in greaseproof paper. But when they reached the hollow oak in which the bees had taken up residence – oh, many years ago, long before the days of Pooh and Christopher Robin – Pooh looked at the oak and then at Christopher Robin and then back at the oak.

"Do you see what I don't see, Christopher Robin?"

"Yes, Pooh. Or no, as the case may be."

There were no bees in the hollow oak. Christopher Robin and Pooh walked around the tree several times

and into it and out of it again. There was nothing except a few wood lice.

"Let's look on the bright side," said Christopher Robin.

"Is there a bright side?"

"Of course there is, Pooh. Here we are with several slices of bread-and-butter and nobody to eat them."

"Well, there is somebody to eat them," said Pooh, "and that is certainly a bright side, but, on the dark side, if there are no bees . . ."

"I was thinking of that myself, Pooh."

"Oh dear," said Pooh.

"Cheer up, Pooh."

Christopher Robin handed him a piece of bread-and-butter. "We will organise a Search Party."

"I don't think I am feeling very well," said Pooh, passing the bread-and-butter back to Christopher Robin. "I shall go home and count my pots of honey."

But when he reached home, another shock awaited him. There were only three pots in the cupboard. And it didn't take him long to count to three. When he looked more closely it appeared that one of them was empty. There was nothing for it but to compose a sad hum. It went like this:

Piglet had a haycorn,
A nice, big round one.
Eeyore had a thistle,
Which was juicy and green.
Rabbit had a carrot
(He went out and found one)
Which was all very well for him.

Pooh looked everywhere,
The bedroom, the kitchen,
Even in the corners of the garden shed,
But there wasn't any honey,
Not a spoonful, not a smidgeon.
"I should have stayed in bed,"
Said Pooh,
"With blankets on my head."

So Piglet, enjoy
Your fine, round haycorn,
Eeyore, your thistle
So juicy and green,
And Rabbit eat your carrot
And I hope that you enjoy it
While Pooh grows sad and lean.

For there isn't any honey,
In the pot or in the larder,
And I even had a look in the gloomy shed.
No, there isn't any honey,
And it isn't very funny.
"I should have stayed in bed,"
Said Pooh,
"And just *dreamt* of honey instead."

But this hum depressed Pooh even more. He tried to imagine a world without honey and how difficult it would be to get out of bed in the morning knowing that the shelf would be empty. And how difficult it would be to go to sleep at night knowing that when he got up again things would be just the same! He could only think of one way to cheer himself up. Very slowly he put a paw on the second-to-last pot of honey, and very slowly he drew it to him.

*   *   *

Meanwhile, Christopher Robin had set off on a tour of the Forest to ask if anyone had seen the bees. He started in the boggy place that was home to Eeyore.

"Lost your way, Christopher Robin?"

"No, Eeyore, I came to see you."

"That's very kind of you. Of course, I do have other visitors from time to time. A week ago last Thursday there was this hedgehog, but hedgehogs, well, they've not got much small talk. One does one's best. 'How are the prickles?' I ask. 'Much the same,' they say, and then the conversation dries up."

"I came to ask you something. Eeyore, have you seen any bees? They've gone missing."

"Oh, they have, have they? Well, they haven't come here. They've swarmed, I expect. That's what bees do. The grass is always greener on the other side of the Forest. Would have swarmed myself years ago, but it's not the sort of thing one can do on one's own."

"Oh, Eeyore, thank you. You've been such a help."

"Really?" asked Eeyore to Christopher Robin's retreating back. "You're not just saying that? Glad to have been of service, if I was. And if not, think nothing of it. Come again in a year or two."

"Owl," said Christopher Robin a short time later, "we're looking for the bees."

"They'll be in the hollow oak," said Owl.

"We thought so too, but they really aren't, and Eeyore thinks they may have swarmed to somewhere else. Owl, I was wondering, if you were to fly over the Forest you might spot them, then hoot for us to come over."

"Indeed," conceded Owl. He really wanted to say something else, only Christopher Robin seemed to have covered it all already.

Pausing only to exercise his wings with a few loosening flaps, off Owl went. He flew east into the sun, which made him blink, south to where he could see his shadow flying beneath him on the chalky slopes of the downs, west to Where the Woozle Wasn't (and where the bees weren't either), and then back north to where he had started from. Everywhere there were trees and rolling grass and little insects – none of which were bees.

He was considering Giving Up and going home to a mug of cocoa and a digestive biscuit when he saw what at first he took to be a bundle of bracken in a bush, or maybe a pile of old leaves rolled along by the wind into a place from which they could roll no further.

Owl thought to himself: "Maybe," and then, "It might be!" and then, "It is!" He hooted his loudest hoot and Christopher Robin, hearing him, climbed onto his

bicycle and tinkled the bell. Pooh balanced himself in the bicycle basket and directed Christopher Robin all the way to where Owl was hovering on a friendly current of air. Sure enough, in a bramble bush right underneath Owl was what might have been a bundle of bracken or a pile of old leaves, but was neither of those things. Pooh's eyes opened very wide.

"Bees," he cried. "Thousands and thousands of them."

"Oh, Pooh!" said Christopher Robin, one foot on the ground to steady the bicycle. "Aren't they grand?"

"Should I ask them to come home?" asked Pooh.

"You could try."

"Bees!" cried Pooh. The bees buzzed a little louder. "BEES!"

The buzzing of the bees grew not just louder but angrier and one of them landed on Pooh's nose.

"I don't think this is working, Pooh. We shall have to think of something else," said Christopher Robin.

"I can only think of honey," said Pooh sadly, "and having none." He blew the bee off his nose.

They moved away from the swarm, and then stopped to think.

"Perhaps they don't like our voices," suggested Christopher Robin.

"I can't help being growly," said Pooh. "I'm a Bear."

"We could play them some music," said Christopher Robin.

"*The Homecoming Waltz*, perhaps. I'll go and get the gramophone."

But the bees ignored *The Homecoming Waltz*; and when Christopher Robin played *God Save the King* the

buzzing became Very Fierce indeed, and Pooh said: "Maybe it should be *God Save the Queen*?" but they didn't have that.

Then, when Christopher Robin put on *You Are My Honeysuckle, I Am The Bee*, the buzzing got so ferocious that Pooh took the needle off the record in such a hurry that it made a big scratch.

"Bother!" said Pooh. "If they don't like conversation and they don't like music, and if they keep getting angry all the time, what are we to do?"

"We must hold a Crisis Meeting," said Christopher Robin. "I'll summon the others."

So Christopher Robin rode off on his bicycle, while Pooh returned home to do an Emergency Check on his pantry. To his dismay, there were only two pots of honey left on the shelf, and one of them was nearly empty. He put them on the table, and he counted them this way and that, but it was not much fun counting to two (or one and a quarter), whichever way you did it. So he put his finger into one of them and took it out and sucked it. He thought he had never tasted anything so delicious in all his life.

The Crisis Meeting was held the next morning in a clearing in the Forest. Pooh explained that the bees had left the hollow oak; Owl described where they had ended up and Christopher Robin suggested that they needed to be Enticed Back. Then there was silence, except for a chomping sound. Lottie, who was seated on the edge of the circle, was making daisy chains, biting through the stalks with her sharp little teeth.

"The thing about bees," she said, when she noticed everyone was looking, "is that they like flowers. And they do what their Queen tells them to, so you need to get her on your side. You can tell which one the Queen Bee is because she makes
a sort of humming noise."

"Lottie, you are a
remarkable rodent!" said
Christopher Robin. "Do
you have a plan?"

"Otters are not rodents but *mustelids* actually," said Lottie. "But, yes, I am remarkable, and I do have a plan."

Then she told them that bees like not only flowers but shiny, glittery things in general, so colourful decorations might entice them back. Everyone was asked to search their houses and the Forest for anything suitable with which to decorate the hollow oak.

Oh, how they toiled! Eeyore trotted to the very edge of the Forest, with Piglet on his back clinging tightly to his mane, and they returned with masses of bluebells and clover. Rabbit summoned as many Friends and Relations as could be brought together at short notice and instructed them to come back with anything that was glittery. Rabbit himself contributed a canteen of cutlery which he had been polishing and keeping for a special occasion. Kanga had taken on the job of arranging things, hanging spoons and forks around the entrance to the hollow part of the tree. Lottie slunk along dragging a diamond tiara.

"It's not real, of course," she explained to anyone who

would listen (and some who would not), "but it comes from a very good house."

Roo and Tigger found a box of marbles which they put into nets, and these too were attached to the tree branches like exotic fruit. Christopher Robin tied the model aeroplane to a twig as high up as he could reach.

By the time the sun had fallen behind the Six Pine Trees the work was finished, and everyone stood back staring in wonder at a tree unlike any that had ever been seen in that Forest or any other. On every twig within reach were wreaths of flowers, and from every branch hung tinkly, glittery things which twisted and turned in the breeze and reflected the crimson sky.

Piglet sighed: "That is beautiful."

"Yes," said Pooh, "but will the bees think so?"

There was nothing for it but to wait until the morning.

Pooh had a dream that night. He was in a cage, and beyond the bars of the cage was a honey tree. It was covered in buds, and from each bud there dripped down a rich, heavy dollop of – oh, my! But whenever he tried to stretch his paws through the bars they were immediately grasped by brambles.

Suddenly he woke up. Through the window he could just see to the east a lightening of the sky, all lemon and pink.

Would the bees be back? Would there be honey?

Pooh's stomach rumbled sadly, but he ignored it and climbed out of bed.

It was so cold at dawn in the Hundred Acre Wood that Pooh could see his breath making smoke signals in the air. He listened hard and could just hear the tinkly, glittery sounds of all the things that were hanging from the tree. He rounded the corner, and there in front of him stood the hollow oak.

But no bees.

"Oh . . . bother," said Pooh, though bother was not quite what he meant. "Oh, double bother!" he added.

He felt as if he should very probably compose a hum; only it was as if the bees had taken all the hums with them. There were no hums left in the world, and no honey and no smackerels of anything, and only empty tummies . . . and while there might be a rhyme or two in all that, Pooh didn't have the heart for it.

"Please come back and make some honey," he said to any bees who might be listening. But, of course, no bee could hear him.

Pooh sat on the ground and stared at the empty, glittering tree. He stared until the sun was high in the sky, and the other animals came to find out if Lottie's plan had worked.

When they saw how things were, they began to remove the decorations from the tree. They took away

the aeroplane, and the marbles, and the baubles, and the spoons and the forks, and the tiara that had glittered so beautifully, although it was only paste.

When they were finished, Christopher Robin said to Pooh: "Don't worry, we'll think of an idea," and he led everyone away.

Pooh didn't go with them, but stood quietly wishing that he was not a Bear of Little Brain and that he could think of an idea himself.

Pooh decided to go back to the bramble bush and check that the swarm was still there, which it was. Then it occurred to him that if he stood on a nearby branch, he might be able to hear the humming noise that Lottie had said the Queen made. Perhaps if a Honeyless Bear bowed very low and asked her very nicely, a Queen might take pity on him.

Still all Pooh could hear was the rustle of leaves. Maybe if he edged a little further, so that his ears were really close to the bees, then . . .

There was a loud crack as the branch on which he was standing gave way. Pooh landed face first, right in the middle of the swarm – and in the brambles.

Then for the first time he heard the humming noise, and he thought to himself that it must be the Queen, but no sooner had he thought this than he felt a sharp pain on the end of his nose. It might have been a sting and it might have been a bramble, but he found that he didn't care which just so long as there weren't any more.

So he picked himself up and ran away as quickly as he could, and the bees flew after him just as fast.

Then, as he ran from the bees thinking about very little except that he was running and a swarm of angry bees was behind him, Pooh found that he had an idea. And it was not just an everyday idea, but one of the very best ideas he had ever had. Instead of running back to his own house, or Christopher Robin's house, or anywhere else at all, he went straight back to the hollow tree.

When he got there, he pretended to hide inside. Sounding crosser than ever, the bees followed him in.

But Winnie-the-Pooh was not there. He had sneaked out by the back way and sat on a little hillock about a hundred yards away, to see whether the bees would follow him out.

He watched and he watched, but although all the bees had flown into the tree not a single one flew out. And when he had satisfied himself that the bees were back to stay, he forgot about how sore and swollen his nose was and how cold it was when you had had no breakfast and had forgotten your scarf, and he began to think about his bed, which would be nice and warm. Better still, he thought of his one remaining pot of honey, which had still not been opened.

But it soon would be.

·CHAPTER SIX·

*in which Owl becomes an author,
and then unbecomes one*

IT WAS A WINDY, BREEZY SORT OF MORNING, with the clouds scurrying across the sky as if there was a reward waiting for them at the horizon, and the tops of the trees bending excitedly this way and that. Things, it seemed, were On the Move.

Outside Owl's house (which was really Piglet's house because Owl's house had blown down and – well, you remember), Tigger and Roo  were playing a new game which each claimed to have invented. It was called Falling Leaves. You grabbed a handful of leaves and threw them into the air

and had to make sure that you were
not there when they came down again.
If a leaf landed on you or even touched
your arm you had to do a forfeit,
and any game with forfeits is sure
to be exciting.

Tigger was standing on his head and singing *Twinkle Twinkle Little Star* backwards as a forfeit for getting a leaf caught in his whiskers, when Owl came swooping down out of an upstairs window. He hooted angrily, pulled Tigger's tail so that he fell over, and boxed Roo's ears.

"He did it really hard," complained Roo, as Owl flew back to his house.

"He wouldn't like it if *I* pulled *his* tail," said Tigger. "What's got into him? He's even grumpier than usual."

"Don't know," said Roo. "Race you to the Six Pine Trees!"

Owl was busy. If you were to knock on his door and wait for a while you might be lucky or, more likely, not. If Owl did come to the door and you were to ask him: "What are you up to these days?"

he would look mysterious and say: "Mind your own business," or "You wouldn't understand," or "Don't want any today, thank you very much."

The animals and Christopher Robin discussed what Owl might be up to. Rabbit thought it must be something big.

"Perhaps he's spring cleaning," suggested Kanga.

"You don't think the Thesaurus has got him, do you?" Piglet said anxiously.

"Well, let's find out," said Christopher Robin.

So they went to Owl's house and Christopher Robin tugged the bell-pull eight times until it came away in his hand and then banged on the door with the sole of his shoe.

"Owl," he shouted through the door, "we are going to have a picnic. Do you want to come along?"

"No!" said a cross voice from within.

"How about a row up the river to say hallo to the swans?"

"Don't like swans. Noisy, vulgar things."

Then, when Christopher Robin shouted, "Open the door, Owl, I've got a present for you" (which wasn't really true but is a good way of getting people to open doors when they don't want to), Owl replied: "Not interested. Busy."

It was Piglet who uncovered the mystery. He scrambled around to the back of Owl's house and peered through a gap in the curtains, and there was Owl sucking the end of his quill pen.

"He looked as if he was writing a book," said Piglet, "but I didn't actually see him *write* anything."

"We must get him out of the house," said Rabbit. "It can't be healthy, cooped up like that. We could try smoking him out."

"We could starve him out," said Piglet, and then he added: "Just a little."

"Perhaps we could deliver a large wooden horse to him," said Christopher Robin, "and have somebody hiding inside . . . no, that wouldn't work."

"I've got it. We will burrow under his house," said Rabbit, "and get in that way."

So Rabbit, aided by Friends and Relations, burrowed under Owl's house and made an opening just big enough for Lottie to wriggle through.

She waited until she heard Owl going into the pantry, and then came up underneath the rug in his study.

There was nothing particularly odd in the room, except a big pile of papers on Owl's desk. Lottie took the top sheet between her teeth and pulled it out through the burrow to show to the others.

"It's got writing on it," said Rabbit, in case they hadn't noticed.

Christopher Robin looked at the sheet of paper. This is what it said:

UNCUL ROBERT

A LEJEND IN HIS LIFETIME

BY WOL

"Ooh, show it to me, show it to me!" cried Piglet, who never liked to be left out of things, except, sometimes, buckets that were going down wells.

"What Owl is writing," said Christopher Robin, "is the story of his Uncle Robert."

"That's still no reason to pull my tail," said Tigger.

"Or box my ears," Roo added, "which isn't funny."

The very next day Christopher Robin met Owl, who was cutting back the branches that were growing over his window.

"Hallo, Owl," said Christopher Robin. "You're writing a book?"

"Oh, so you know," said Owl. "It's a monograph."

"I'm not sure what that is, Owl."

"It's the story of my late Uncle Robert, who lived in Pretoria."

"Was he always late?" asked Christopher Robin. "Even for dinner?"

"You will have to read the book when it's published," said Owl loftily, "and now if you'll excuse me —" And he disappeared into his house.

The following morning, Christopher Robin and Pooh were at Christopher Robin's house having their elevenses: squashed-fly biscuits for Christopher Robin and condensed milk for Pooh. They had just started to listen to some music on the gramophone, and Pooh was wondering where the musicians were, and how they knew to start playing when you put the needle on the record, when Rabbit came in noisily.

"We're going to have to do something about Owl," he said.

"Are we?" asked Christopher Robin. "Have a biscuit, Rabbit."

"There's no time for biscuits. Owl is not the Owl he was."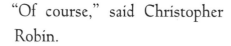

"Biscuits don't take long," Pooh commented. "Unless you get crumbs in your bed."

"I expect he'll get over it," said Christopher Robin, putting on a new record.

"No, no, no," said Rabbit, impatiently.

Then suddenly he had an idea, and knew that it was one of the finest ideas the Forest had ever known.

"May I borrow your gramophone, Christopher Robin?" he asked.

"Of course," said Christopher Robin.

"Thank you," said Rabbit, then he looked severely at Pooh. "Everyone will assemble outside my house after luncheon, and I will explain my plan."

That evening, Owl settled down to write *Chapter 1: Wer and Wen Uncul Robert was Bron*. It was a chapter he had started to write a good many times, and he had just written *Uncul Robert was bron* one more time when he thought he deserved a break, so he got up to fetch himself a glass of fizzy lemonade and stretch his wings a bit.

However, as he passed the living room window he saw outside it a placard. There was writing on the placard, and the writing said:

I DONT WANT YOU TO RITE MY STORY
(SIGNED) UNCUL ROBERT

"Ah, phooey!" said Owl. And then he shouted: "You out there! I know who you are and I shall come out and box your ears."

But he did not leave his house nor box any more ears, but went rather thoughtfully to fetch the lemonade. While he was out of the room, something slinky and slithery crept from underneath the rug and a little later slinked and slithered back again, just before Owl returned.

Having flapped his wings a few times, Owl resumed his writing position, but there on top of page one was a large sign. It read:

I MENE IT!!!

"Oh, really," said Owl, "this is too much." He lifted up his quill and sucked on the end of it, but before he could write another word a ghostly voice, unlike any voice that Owl had ever heard before, echoed from the chimney.

"Owl," it said. "Nephew Owl. I do not want you to write this book."

"Who is that and where are you?" Owl asked nervously.

"It is your late Uncle Robert from Beyond the Grave."

"I don't believe you," said Owl, but his voice trembled a little as he said it.

"You'd better," said the Voice, "or you will regret it."

At that moment there was a loud rumble of thunder, or possibly it was a sheet of corrugated iron being shaken.

"If you really are my Uncle Robert," said Owl, and he had to clear his throat several times before he spoke, "prove it. Tell me what you did every night before you went to bed."

At this there was quite a lengthy pause before the Voice said (in a rather hesitant and unconvincing way), "I said my prayers."

"No, you didn't," said Owl. "You drank a whisky."

"I drank a whisky and *then* I said my prayers," said the Voice.

Owl considered this, but before he could think of a suitable answer the Voice added, now sounding quite like Rabbit: "If you continue writing this book, you will wish you had not."

"Stuff and nonsense!" said Owl, very rudely, and sat back down at his desk.

But just then a loud blast of music resounded from the chimney. It was the National Anthem, so Owl had to stand to attention until it was over. And the music played and the thunder rumbled and outside the window a paw held up a placard reading *DONT!!!* and the Voice from the chimney said "BE WARNED! BE WARNED!" and several small animals covered

in sheets came out from under the rug crying "WHOO WHOO!" and pretending to be ghosts.

Then Owl thought that he had had quite enough, and flew out of the upstairs window into the branches of another tree. He sat there in the dark for quite a long time, until finally the noises stopped.

A twig snapped loudly.

"Bother," said someone.

"Go away, if you are there!" shouted Owl. "And if you aren't, you can still go away!"

Once more there was silence, until Owl concluded that it was silly to be sitting in a tree and shouting at the darkness, so he flew back indoors. But the funny thing was that when at last Owl went to bed (after saying his prayers, which he never usually did), he lay awake thinking.

His head was buzzing with a jumble of placards and patriotic music and things in sheets and thunder and a suspicion that he might have behaved rather foolishly. And

the more he thought he should stop writing his book just to be on the safe side, the more he thought he shouldn't stop writing it, because that would be Giving In.

"Shan't!" he said very loudly to the darkness, and then he fell asleep.

Meanwhile, in another part of the wood, the others were saying goodnight to one another. Tigger returned the corrugated iron to the roof of Kanga's shed, and the Friends and Relations folded up their sheets and gave them back to Rabbit. Everyone was starting to wonder if they had done the right thing, and whether Christopher Robin would quite like it when he heard. After all, did it matter whether Owl wrote a book or not?

Piglet said: "I think it was quite clever of him to write as much as he did."

"But he shouldn't have boxed my ears," Roo insisted.

"Or pulled my tail," agreed Tigger.

"I expect he knows that now," said Piglet.

"I don't suppose he will do it again," said Pooh.

"Quite so," said Rabbit. "Quite, quite so."

And indeed, Owl seemed to have got over his fright very well.

For a few days afterwards, if people came up to him and asked him how he was getting on with his book he would say defiantly: "Very well. I've got to the bit when he takes up fire-walking." Or "I'm just working on his days in the animal hospital." Or "He's at the Siege of Mafeking this week."

But in time, people stopped asking. Roo and Tigger resumed their games of Falling Leaves outside Owl's house and nobody boxed their ears or pulled their tails, which they were pleased about even though it made the game less exciting.

Then one day, Rabbit decided to visit Owl, and to take some old letters that Uncle Robert had sent to Grandad Buck, because goodness knows Rabbit didn't need them cluttering up the place.

"I thought these might be useful for your writing," said Rabbit, when a glaring Owl met him at the door. "Going well, is it?"

"Write? Me?" snapped Owl. "You must be muddling me up with someone else. Now, I am extremely busy, so if –" he paused and blinked. "How fascinating!" he cried, snatching an envelope from Rabbit.

"Is that a Twopenny Blue? An extremely rare stamp," continued Owl, bustling over to his desk, where a large album was surrounded by piles of old envelopes. "Do take a seat, and if you promise to pay attention I will show you my collection."

Rabbit sighed and sat down, glancing longingly at the door. Owl began to tell Rabbit all about his stamp collection and all the different countries the stamps came from. He went on telling him about it for hours and hours, until Rabbit had had enough and remembered an urgent appointment.

And that was the first of many such days that summer when Rabbit tried to stay awake and look interested while Owl went on about his stamps, until eventually Rabbit would suddenly remember something very important he had to do.

But even Owl's enthusiasm for his stamps declined in time and in later years, when the woodworm had gnawed halfway through the leg of Owl's bed, the stamp album served splendidly as a prop.

And one cold night, when Owl needed a draught excluder, the unfinished book came in very useful, too.

·CHAPTER SEVEN·

in which Lottie starts an Academy,
and everybody learns something

"DID YOU MISS US when you were away at school?"
Pooh asked Christopher Robin one August
morning when the Hundred Acre Wood was at
its best.

"I did," said Christopher Robin, "but then something
would happen and I would forget. It's noisy at school.
Everyone shouts."

"It's very noisy in the Forest too," said Pooh.

"Yes, but here the noises come one at a time, and at
school they all come together."

Pooh seemed to be a little disappointed with
Christopher Robin's answer.

"If you don't miss us, nobody will."

"Silly old Bear," said Christopher Robin. "I might not
have missed you all the time, but I never forgot you."

Pooh nodded slowly. Then he brightened, and suggested: "Maybe we should have a school here, and you could be the head master."

"What a good idea," said Christopher Robin. "Only I'm not old enough to be a head master, and I haven't got a gown." Then he thought for a moment, and added, "But I wonder . . ."

Meanwhile, over in the place that had been boggy before it turned dry and crusty, Lottie was swimming around in her old tin trunk, Fortitude Hall, and explaining to Eeyore what was wrong with the Forest.

"Perhaps, since you have been here such a very long time, Eeyore, you don't notice things as clearly as I do. But it seems to me that the behaviour of some of the animals is Quite Uncouth."

"Especially the stripy ones," agreed Eeyore.

"Exactly. Stripes or spots, fur or feathers, what they need is a little discipline. So I have a Proposition to put to you."

"Well, let me get comfortable first," said Eeyore, scratching that place behind his right ear where a scratch was always welcome.

At exactly this moment, Christopher Robin and Pooh came into view.

Christopher Robin was riding his bicycle, and Pooh was perched on the crossbar. At least, some of the time he was. Christopher Robin could not see the grass in front of him, because Pooh was in the way. So every time they went over a tussock, the bear was bumped into the air and tumbled on to the ground.

"I'm not sure that bicycles were meant for bears, or bears for bicycles," said Pooh, getting down carefully as Christopher Robin stopped beside Lottie's trunk. Pooh rubbed that part of him which was meant for landing on, but which had been landed on rather too much.

Christopher Robin gave him a consoling pat.

"Why don't you tell them about our proposal," he suggested.

"We have a proposal too!" said Lottie. "Shall we go first?"

"I think we should go at the same time," said Christopher Robin. "One, two, three –"

"What the Forest needs is a school," said Lottie, and at the same time Pooh said: "We were thinking of a school in the Forest."

"How strange," said Eeyore. "There seems to be a sort of echo around here."

The four of them went and sat in a magic ring of mushrooms, which is the best place in a Forest to have ideas, and sure enough their plans came thick and fast. Owl was the obvious choice to teach Latin and Greek, Rabbit would be asked to take Household Management, and Kanga, Geography.

"What will you teach, Lottie?" asked Christopher Robin.

"I shall teach Good Manners, Dancing and Deportment, Elocution and Water Sports. Diverse subjects, but I am skilled in them all."

"I shall take sports," said Christopher Robin, "and throwing the cricket ball. But we'll need a head master. I thought that maybe –"

At just the same time Lottie lowered her voice and said a little huskily: "I thought maybe you, Eeyore . . ."

There was a long pause. Eeyore shuffled his feet.

"Could you mean me, Lottie? Eeyore, the old grey donkey, head master of a school?"

"Yes!" said Lottie, Pooh and Christopher Robin together.

It was so quiet in the Forest you could almost hear the spiders knitting their cobwebs.

At length Eeyore said: "I shall need a gown, a mortar board and a blackboard. And plenty of chalk. It often breaks, you know."

"Excellent," said the otter. "You shall be head master of – yes, let us call it the Hundred Acre Wood Academy!"

So that was settled, and Lottie went to carry the news to the others.

When she asked Owl to teach Latin, he stretched his wings a couple of times, then intoned: "The verb *amare*, which means 'to love', is declined: *amo, amare, amavi, amatum*."

"Just what I had in mind," said Lottie, and she hurried outside, where Tigger and Roo could be heard beginning

an energetic game. Tigger tried to bounce out of her way, but Lottie was too fast for him, and before he knew it he had agreed to be a pupil.

"As long as Roo comes too!" he added belatedly.

Roo looked uncertain and said he would be a pupil as long as Piglet came too, and wouldn't Lottie like to ask Piglet first? Unfortunately for Roo, Piglet happened to stroll by at that very moment and, when he was asked, said: "I'll come! I do want to know things, Roo, because there are so many things I don't know – more than a hundred!"

"Oh," said Roo. "Well, I know seven times four, and the capital of Spain, but I'm not telling you."

*   *   *

On the first day of term, the four pupils of the Hundred Acre Wood Academy presented themselves right in the middle of the Hundred Acre Wood, where Eeyore was standing in front of a blackboard. He was wearing a mortar board and a

fine old gown with a scarlet
hood, and held a new piece of
yellow chalk in one hoof and one
of those things for rubbing out
blackboard chalk in another. He
welcomed the pupils by reading
the register (which didn't take
long), then handed it solemnly to
Pooh, who had been recruited as Prefect and given
an armband that Kanga had made especially for him.
It said PERFECT on it, and Pooh was so busy admiring
it that he dropped the register.

Eeyore rolled his eyes, cleared his throat, and wrapped
his gown closer around him. A couple of moths flew out.

"I am your head master," he announced. "Now, do you all have your schoolbooks and pencils? Yes? Then I shall write on the board the school motto, and you are to copy it onto page one of your schoolbooks. The motto is –" The chalk scratched and squeaked as Eeyore wrote the word 'FLOREAT'. "Owl, our Classics Master, will translate for us."

Owl had not expected this, but said in a deep voice: "*Floreat*. Do not leave your hat on the floor."

"We haven't got hats," said Tigger.

"There isn't a floor," said Piglet.

"I want a hat. Can I have a hat? Can it have ribbons on it?" cried Roo, getting more and more excited.

"Settle down everybody," said Pooh the Perfect. "It's time for assembly."

"We're assembled already," Piglet pointed out.

"Then pay attention!" said Eeyore severely. "Now, in a lifetime in the Hundred Acre Wood, I have learned a few tips which I shall pass on to you. One: do not expect thistles always to be crisp and juicy. Sometimes they are crisp, and sometimes they are –"

At this point there was an audible Tiggerish whisper: "They are hot, hot, hot!"

"– juicy," finished Eeyore, ignoring Tigger magnificently.

"Two: if there is a boggy patch and you have clean feet you will step into the boggy patch, as sure as eggs is eggs, or my name isn't Eeyore. Three –" Eeyore seemed unsure for a moment. "Three: eggs is eggs. And four: my name certainly is Eeyore, and don't you forget it. Now, off with the lot of you to class."

And so the schooling began. The first lesson was Household Management, where Rabbit tried to explain a list of Things That Should Be Folded (napkins, tablecloths, sheets) as against

Things That Really Should Not (hardboiled eggs, cobwebs, desks).

Then they were all treated to Owl's Latin class, where he declined *amo, amas, amat* for them several times, and told them that *mus* is the Latin for 'mouse', but became rather short-tempered when Pooh asked whether 'hus' was the Latin for 'house'

and Piglet wanted to know if 'puss' was the Latin for 'cat'.

Things were little better in Geography, where Kanga tried to explain that the

Equator was an Imaginary Line that Ran All Around the World.

Piglet put his paw in the air.

"Please, Kanga, if the line is imaginary, how do we know it's there?" he asked.

"Roo dear, don't put your pencil up your nose," said Kanga. "Now, Piglet, that's just it. We don't know the line is there."

"In that case," said Tigger, "why mention it?"

"Because if I didn't mention it, you wouldn't know about it!" responded Kanga rather briskly.

Roo said: "But you don't know about it either."

Kanga could be seen counting to ten under her breath.

"Of course I do, I'm your mother," she informed Roo. "Now, children, it's time for break!"

*   *   *

While the pupils were having their break, the teachers met to discuss why there wasn't any discipline.

"It's the stripy ones," said Eeyore gloomily, shaking another moth out of his gown, which he had taken off because of the heat.

"It's all of them," said Rabbit, twitching his nose. "Really, I thought Roo would have been better brought up!"

Kanga gave him a warning look. "And what do you mean by that, Rabbit?"

Owl cleared his throat.

"The gravity of the situation means, suggests, connotes, imports and portends –" he paused for a moment, looking rather as if he had forgotten what he was saying. "It means we need Christopher Robin!" he concluded, recovering splendidly.

But Lottie was having none of that.

"Nonsense!" she snorted. "He's not due until after lunch. I can deal with this."

After the break, Lottie taught Dancing and Deportment.

"I hear that you have not been living up to the high standards of the Academy," she told the pupils as they stood in line in front of her.

"Sorry, Lottie," they chorused together, with the exception of Tigger, who was trying to see if he could stick his tail into his ear.

"Pooh, as Prefect it is your duty to assist the teachers in Keeping Order," the otter continued.

"Yes, Lottie," agreed Pooh, trying to sound as clever as he could, and wondering if Keeping Order could mean putting your honey pots in a very neat row and then staying at home to guard them.

"I am here to teach you good manners and grace," said Lottie. "And we shall begin with the polka, a lively yet refined dance. Imagine, if you will, a grand ballroom filled with the crowned heads of Europe: dashing men in uniform and beautiful women in flowing silks."

Here she placed a record carefully onto the gramophone, which she had borrowed from Christopher Robin.

"Are you all partnered? Piglet and Tigger, Pooh and Roo? Now, follow my lead – in time with the music! One, two, three, hop! – that's it – one, two, three, hop! – no, Tigger, hop, not bounce – no, Tigger, no, no, NO!"

But it was too late. Tigger, holding Piglet in his paws, had bounced high up into the air. And when they came down again, it was on top of Lottie.

"You're squishing me!" squeaked Piglet from in between Tigger and Lottie.

"One, two, three, hop," continued Pooh as he polkaed past the pile, deep in concentration, not noticing that he had trodden on Roo's feet three times and Tigger's twice.

"Desist!" shouted Lottie as her head appeared from underneath Tigger's tummy. With a twist of her powerful tail, she managed to extricate herself from the heap. She drew herself up to her full height in front of Pooh.

Pooh stopped short.

"Do you want me to – what was it – insist?" he asked nervously.

"Lunch!" Lottie cried. "Lunch, everybody!"

* * *

Pooh kept the pupils busy with sandwiches and the school song until the games master himself arrived.

At once, the staff of the Hundred Acre Wood Academy told him of their difficulties.

Christopher Robin listened gravely, and did not laugh, though perhaps the corner of his mouth twitched a little, once or twice.

"Well, Tigger always was more of an outdoor type," was all he said.

After lunch, Christopher Robin took charge of the sports. First, he organised a High Jump. Piglet ran up to the bar . . . and then ran under it. The High Jump was easily won by Tigger, who jumped not only over the bar but the posts as well.

"Well done, Tigger!" cried everybody, except Eeyore, who remarked: "It looked more like a bounce to me."

Then it was time for the Long Jump. Piglet ran up to the sandpit, but instead of jumping made a fine sandcastle with a bucket that he had found lying about, the way buckets do. The Long Jump was won by Roo, who jumped right to the far end of the sandpit and beyond.

"Well jumped, Roo!" cried Kanga.

And after all that, when the animals were flushed and panting, Christopher Robin sat them all down, the pupils on one side and the  teachers on the other, and asked them how they had liked school.

There was a very long pause, and then everyone talked at once.

"An interesting experiment," suggested Owl.

"*Amo*, a mouse, a mat, what kind of a language is that?" asked Piglet.

"All that folding and polishing," grumbled Tigger. "Boring!"

"Dancing might be all right if Pooh looked where he's going," squeaked Roo.

"Why does a school have to have pupils anyway?" asked Lottie.

There was another pause.

"By the way, I can't teach at all next week," said Kanga. "It's my spring cleaning, you know."

"Mine too," said Rabbit.

"That's a shame," said Christopher Robin. "What about everyone else?"

But suddenly it seemed that nobody at all was available anymore. Nor did anyone seem to mind.

Pooh had said nothing against school, because he was a Perfect. But a few days later, when they were having elevenses at his house, and Pooh was hoping Christopher Robin would hurry up so that they weren't late for twelvses, he found himself saying: "I didn't really want to go to school, you know."

"Oh?" prompted Christopher Robin, buttering toast.

"It didn't seem the right sort of thing to do on a sunny day. But . . . but . . ." He wanted to add something about being a Perfect, and not being one any longer and how school had been . . . well . . .

"I feel the same way myself sometimes," said Christopher Robin carelessly. "By the way, though, the thing about being a Prefect is, you don't stop being one when you're not at school."

"You don't?" said Pooh, so interested that the pawful of honey stopped halfway to his mouth.

"So I was going to mention that you ought really to go on wearing your armband, at least on special occasions. Sort of like soldiers and medals."

So Winnie-the-Pooh did just that. And he was not the only one. If you visited Eeyore when he wasn't expecting you, you would sometimes find him in his gown and mortar board, using the tassle to keep flies away, and the blackboard to practise his tap-dancing.

And as for Lottie, she could not keep her mind on anything for very long, and when Piglet asked her a week or so later about the Academy, she answered: "Academy, darling? What do you mean?"

Otters are like that.

·CHAPTER EIGHT·

in which we are introduced
to the game of cricket

CHRISTOPHER ROBIN had had a birthday. There had been cards with laughing kittens wishing him a happy day, and the usual presents: socks and gloves and writing paper and a fat book called *1001 Things to Do in the Holidays*.

Christopher Robin had used the writing paper to write letters saying thank you for the socks and the gloves. He had not found this easy, thinking that a letter saying:

> *Dear Whoever,*
> *Thank you for the socks/gloves.*
> *Yours sincerely,*
> *Christopher Robin*

would have done the job nicely, but it seemed that people wanted bits about the weather and where he had come in maths, and *I do hope you are well.*

Having put the socks and gloves in the very back of the drawer, he turned to 1001 *Things to Do in the Holidays.* On page three it suggested clearing out the potting shed, and on page five it suggested putting toys in boxes with sticky labels on them, and on page seven it suggested: 'Why not make a list of all the people you most admire from your history books?'

Christopher Robin did not know what it said on page nine, because after reading page seven he had closed the book and never opened it again.

But there had been one present that he had liked very much.

This had been a cricket bat, a cricket ball, and two sets of stumps with bails that assembled into a wicket. There was also a pair of batting  gloves, some shin pads, a pair of wicket-keeping gloves, a scoring book with pencils, a pencil sharpener, an eraser, a tin of linseed oil and some squares of cotton for rubbing the oil into the bat. All of which fitted very neatly into a splendid sausage-shaped bag. Everything you needed to play cricket.

This time, when he wrote his thank-you letter, he had added pictures in coloured crayons, and his batting average for the past two summers, and signed the letter, *Love from Christopher Robin.* And he meant it, too.

On this particular day – it may have been a Tuesday, because it often was – he brought the bag to a clearing in the Forest halfway between his house and Owl's house and set up the stumps and the bails on a patch of ground which was not too bumpy. Then he went around the edge of the playing area with a bag of stones, laying them

out to mark the boundary. It was not long before most of the others had gathered around, and Christopher Robin began to explain the rules: "Cricket is a game between two teams. Each team bats once – that's called an innings – and tries to score as many runs as possible.

"The batter faces the bowler from the opposite team, who bowls the ball at him like this." Christopher Robin turned his arm and opened his fingers as if he was letting a ball fly out of his hand. "If he hits the ball, the batter sprints towards where the bowler was standing, and back again. If he reaches the bowler, he scores a run, and if he gets back to where he started from he scores another. If the ball goes right outside the boundary without bouncing, he's scored six runs. But if it bounces, then he only gets four."

"That's easy," said Piglet. "You could just keep going backwards and forwards and getting loads of runs."

"Ah, yes, but the other team is trying to stop you. If you miss the ball and it knocks over your stumps, you're out. If you hit the ball and one of the fielders catches it before it bounces, then you're out too. The same goes if the fielder throws the ball and hits the stumps while you are running. When all the first team is out, everyone changes places, and the batters become the bowlers and fielders."

"Seems like a lot of running up and down," said Eeyore, "for no very good purpose."

"No, no," said Christopher Robin, getting excited. "You see, it's like this . . ."

So he told them more strange things, about having a Short Leg and a Silly Point, and Run-Outs and when a ball was a no-ball and things like that. And while the animals felt that this cricket business was not entirely sensible, they definitely started to get the idea that it was fun.

Over the next few days, from morning until night, while the bees buzzed contentedly around the hollow oak and the gentle whine of an aeroplane looping the loop above the Hundred Acre Wood throbbed in the scented air, it was cricket, cricket and ever more cricket.

Finally, Kanga, who had relatives in Australia, proposed that a proper match should be arranged and that it should be a Test Match. Pooh asked what that was.

Christopher Robin said: "A Test Match is a very important game played between England and Australia. The winner gets the Ashes."

"What ashes are those?" asked Rabbit.

"I'm not quite sure, Rabbit."

"I've got the ashes of my Uncle Robert in a vase on my mantelpiece," said Owl. "It blew over in the great gale and the vase broke, but I got a new vase and most of the ashes."

"I think we should have a Test Match," said Kanga. "Me and Roo can be Australia and the rest of you can be England."

"There can't be just the two of you," said Christopher Robin, "that wouldn't be fair at all."

"We're very good," said Roo. "Really we are. Watch me, watch me!" Saying which, he swung the bat in the air and fell over backwards as he aimed it at the ball. "That was just a practice swing!" he explained, and tried again and fell over backwards again.

"If there were just the two of you, with one of you bowling and one of you keeping wicket, there would be nobody left to field," said Christopher Robin. "I need to think about this."

He went to sit on a large boulder, which was an excellent place to think because it was just the right height and did not interrupt. Eventually he climbed down, and announced: "We will have a Test Match, but we won't be playing for the ashes of Owl's Uncle Robert and it won't be England against Australia. The match will be between the four-legged and the two-legged animals. It will be held on the day after tomorrow and will begin at eleven."

"Cricket under the trees and having fun. Count me out," grumbled Eeyore.

"But, Eeyore," said Pooh. "We won't be able to manage without you."

Eeyore raised an eyebrow.

"These are the teams," continued Christopher Robin. "The Four Legs: Pooh, Tigger, Rabbit and Piglet. The Two Legs: Kanga, Roo and me. Owl is to be the umpire."

"I will captain the Four Legs team," said Rabbit immediately, while some of the others counted their legs.

Lottie cleared her throat. "Excuse me," she said quietly.

"Oh, Lottie, I am sorry," said Christopher Robin, but the truth of it was that he couldn't remember whether Lottie had four legs or two, and it seemed rude to look.

"I know my legs are quite short," Lottie continued, "but that is the way with otters. There are four of them and they have been much admired."

"Of course, Lottie," said Christopher Robin, "I was only hesitating because the Four Legs already outnumber the Two Legs."

"Then I shall play for the Two Legs of course," said Lottie.

After Christopher Robin had thought about it, and Rabbit had got tired of waiting and had gone to clear out the larder – there was never much in it because he liked

it to be clean – and Pooh had had several smackerels of honey and Piglet had become quite pink with excitement thinking about the match and Tigger had had a swallow of the linseed oil and not cared for it at all, a team sheet was produced with the teams set out impressively like this:

FOUR LEGS	TWO LEGS
Tigger	Kanga
Pooh	Roo
Piglet	Lottie (who actually has 4)
Rabbit (captain)	C. Robin (captain)
Eeyore (wicket-keeper)	Eeyore (wicket-keeper)

Umpire: Owl (his decision is final)
Scorers: Henry Rush and Friends and Relations
Too Small to Participate
Extra Fielders: Friends and Relations Big Enough
to Catch a Ball Without Being Squished

"What does the scorer do?" asked Henry Rush, the beetle.

"He adds things up and writes everything down in a book. How is your adding?" said Christopher Robin.

"It's very good some of the time," replied Henry Rush, "but it's difficult when you haven't got fingers."

"Just do your best," said Christopher Robin, patting him gently on the shell.

Christopher Robin made several copies of the team sheet, and decorated them with bats and balls and stumps and bails, and pinned them to the trees around the clearing. Piglet took a copy and showed it to Eeyore.

"It's good, isn't it, Eeyore? We're all on it," he pointed. "This is where it says my name. And your name, Eeyore, is here and here . . ."

"Here *and* here?" enquired Eeyore.

"Yes, Eeyore, because Christopher Robin says you are to be wicket-keeper for both sides."

"A wicked-keeper, little Piglet? Well, well, well." Eeyore did not know what a 'wicked-keeper' was, or what it did, but it sounded necessary.

It was time for the umpire to toss a coin to decide who would bat first. Captain Rabbit had not come back after going to clean his larder, so Tigger was sent to retrieve him, and Pooh was selected as Acting Captain for the Four Legs team.

"Heads or tails?" asked Owl, the umpire.

"I don't know, Owl," said Pooh. "Which is better?"

"Whichever is going to come down on top."

"But I don't know that."

"Which is why I am asking you to guess, Pooh Bear."

Pooh called heads but the coin came down tails up, and Christopher Robin announced that the Two Legs would bat first with Kanga and Lottie opening the innings.

"Where does the wicked-keeper go?" Eeyore asked.

"Behind the wicket, of course," said Christopher Robin. "You have to catch the ball."

"How do I do that?" asked Eeyore, looking at his hooves.

"Any way you can, Eeyore. You have pads and gloves."

"I hardly like to mention this, Christopher Robin, but there only appear to be two pads and others are wearing them."

"You'll just have to do the best you can," said Christopher Robin, who was beginning to think that there was too much talking and not enough playing.

Rabbit, as Captain, made Pooh the bowler, saying he needed the exercise. Lottie hit the first ball of the innings into a clump of heather, and it was only when Friends and Relations joined in the search that the ball was found. At the end of Lottie's first six balls, Henry Rush's scoring team put 30 in the scoring book, under instruction from Rabbit, who kept muttering bad-temperedly: "She's scored three sixes and three fours! Lottie should be on my team."

On his second go at bowling, Pooh became more confident and bowled a couple of really fast ones, the first of which struck Eeyore on the chest.

"Well stopped, Eeyore!" cried Rabbit and there was scattered applause.

"Couldn't help it," wheezed Eeyore.

Then it was Tigger's turn to bowl. He threw the ball high into the air.

"That's called a donkey-drop," said Christopher Robin.

"Not by me," muttered Eeyore.

This time, instead of using the bat to hit the ball, Lottie leapt into the air, twisting and turning, and caught hold of it in mid-flight. Everyone applauded her athleticism but Christopher Robin had to explain that she was not supposed to catch it except when the other side was batting.

"Out!" cried Owl.

"What do you mean by 'Out'?" Lottie went up to Owl, the umpire, and glared at him.

Owl did not react. Christopher Robin explained that if the umpire said you were out he did not need to tell you why.

"You're no gentleman," Lottie told Owl and sulked for a while behind some bluebells, before realising how pretty they looked and picking herself a bunch.

Now it was Kanga's turn to bat. She put Roo into her pouch and when she ran she claimed double the score.

"Both Roo and me," she said.

"Not sure about that," said Owl, and after several such runs judged Roo to be out because his feet had not touched the ground.

When Kanga challenged him, Owl explained: "It says Two Legs, not No Legs. I can't allow any of those runs to count for either of you. And you're out too, Kanga, for arguing with the umpire."

Fortunately for the Two Legs, Christopher Robin was still to bat against Rabbit, and he thwacked the ball for four sixes, one after another, just like that. When Piglet took his turn as bowler he found the ball so heavy that Owl allowed him to run halfway along the pitch before rolling it along the ground. It was Piglet who finally did it for Christopher Robin, bowled out after thirty-three runs.

This was what Henry Rush, with a little help from Christopher Robin, wrote in the smart new scoring book:

TEST MATCH – TWO LEGS VERSUS FOUR LEGS

TWO LEGS INNINGS

Lottie, caught by Lottie	39
Roo, feet off the ground	0
Kanga, arguing with umpire	0
Christopher Robin, bowled by Piglet	33
Extras	3
Total	75

Rabbit and Kanga had spent the morning erecting a sort of shade under the chestnut trees. It consisted of a number of sheets and blankets stitched together. Now, between the two innings, was the time for a refreshing pot of tea and some peppery cucumber sandwiches with the crusts cut off.

While they ate, they discussed the match. Was seventy-five a winning score? Should Owl have given Roo out, or, for that matter, Kanga? How clever of

Piglet to have bowled the ball which knocked over Christopher Robin's wicket.

A little apart from the others stood Eeyore, grumbling as usual: "This wicked-keeping. Standing there and having things thrown at me. A brick wall would do just as well."

"Oh, Eeyore," said Christopher Robin. "We couldn't have a match without you."

"Is that what they're saying, Christopher Robin? Or is it: 'Let the old donkey do it'?"

"Have a cucumber sandwich, Eeyore," suggested Christopher Robin.

"Prefer thistles. More chewy on the whole. Have we finished now, Christopher Robin? Can we go home and nurse our bruises?" asked Eeyore.

"We've finished the first half, Eeyore."

"More, is there? Might have guessed there would be. Still, maybe it will rain."

But it did not even look like raining.

Soon it was time for the Four Legs to take their turn at batting, with seventy-six runs needed to win. Owl slipped on his white umpiring coat and took up his position facing the stumps. Pooh was the first to bat.

Christopher Robin told Kanga to field at a position called Silly Mid-Off and Roo at Silly Mid-On, which meant that Kanga had to glare at Roo for several seconds before he would stop giggling. Then Christopher Robin handed the ball to Lottie.

Twisting and turning as she ran up to bowl, Lottie sent the ball in an arc towards the stumps. When it hit the ground it shot up and caught Pooh on the nose, before falling back and landing on the wicket.

"Out!" said Owl, raising a wing sternly into the air.

"*Ow!*" wailed Pooh.

Then it was Tigger's turn. It didn't take him long to score twenty-seven runs. Then, in his excitement at hitting the ball into a bird's nest in the chestnut tree (they had had to send Owl to fly up and bring it down), Tigger bounced right over the wicket and landed on top of Eeyore.

"How's that?" cried Christopher Robin.

"Painful," gasped Eeyore from underneath Tigger.

"Out. Caught by Eeyore," said Owl.

Rabbit came in to bat, and nudged the ball here, there, and everywhere until he was bowled out by Christopher Robin.

"I thought I'd better give the others a chance," Rabbit commented.

The last in was Piglet, and it was now up to him to score the six runs needed to win the match for the Four Legs. Lottie was to bowl.

During practice, Piglet had found Christopher Robin's birthday bat rather too long and heavy for him to wield, and Rabbit had made him a smaller version out of a cut-down broom handle. But with the first ball from Lottie, Piglet's broom-handle bat shattered.

"*Ow!*" cried Piglet. "That stung! And what will I bat with now?"

"You'll have to use the big one," said Christopher Robin.

"But it's bigger than I am!" worried Piglet.

"Maybe you can hide behind it, little Piglet," said Eeyore.

"I'm sure Lottie won't bowl too fast at you," said Christopher Robin, but there was a glint in Lottie's eye that suggested otherwise.

The otter ran in to bowl.

"I don't want to be here," muttered Piglet, shrinking behind the bat as Lottie approached, looking huge. "I'd much rather be in bed."

The ball, released at great speed by Lottie, landed on the beginnings of a molehill and bounced onto the very edge of Piglet's bat. Piglet dropped the heavy wood with a squawk, but the ball had acquired such momentum that it sailed high into the air and straight over the stones that marked the boundary. A moment of amazed silence was followed by Owl raising his wings and flapping them in the air.

"Six runs," he announced. "Four Legs win the match."

"I did it!" Piglet was hopping up and down in excitement. "I hit a six! I won the game!"

The other players on the Four Legs side, Tigger,

Pooh, Rabbit and Eeyore, gathered around Piglet and raised him high into the air. Christopher Robin, Lottie, Kanga and Roo looked on, smiling despite their disappointment.

"Three cheers for the Four Legs!" cried Christopher Robin. "Hip, hip –"

"Hooray!" cried the others.

"And three more cheers for Piglet!" cried Roo.

So they cheered and cheered some more while Christopher Robin helped Henry Rush and his young assistants to complete the page in the scoring book.

It had a few rubbings out, but looked like this:

FOUR LEGS INNINGS

Pooh, snout before wicket	0
Tigger, caught by Eeyore	27
Rabbit, bowled by Christopher Robin	37
Piglet, not out	6
Extras	6
Total	76

FOUR LEGS WIN!

Late into the evening, everyone sat around a bonfire (the shattered bat had come in useful as kindling) and listened as Christopher Robin told them stories of the great cricketers of past generations.

"But," he added, "in the annals of cricketing legend, whenever and wherever stories are told, they will also mention the mighty six that Piglet hit with a bat taller than he was in the Test Match between the Two Legs and the Four Legs late one summer's afternoon in the Hundred Acre Wood."

"Oh . . ." sighed Piglet happily, as he carelessly toasted a cucumber sandwich. Then he dreamed for a while, until he was roused by Pooh announcing that he had composed a hum to commemorate the occasion.

"I would very much like to hear it," said Lottie who had, after all, been the top scorer of the match.

"So would I," whispered Piglet.

And so here is the hum as hummed by Pooh on the night of the great match, as the eyes of the cricketers shone and glistened in the firelight under the chestnut trees:

Who was it hit the winning run
For the Four Legs against the Two?
Though the bat in his hand
Disappeared into sand,
Was it me?
No –
It was you.

Who was it won the cricket game
For the Four Legs against the Two?
Though his bat was as big
As a fully-grown pig,
Was it me?
No –
It was you.

Do we give a fig for the little pig
And the Four Legs who beat the Two?
We give more than that
For the pig and the bat,
And the mighty hit
Which completed it,
And the mighty swish
Like a massive fish.

Was it me?
No –
It was you.
Not Pooh
But Piglet.
It was you!

"But," said Pooh, "it wasn't really like a fish, only I couldn't think of anything else and then I ran out of time, and sometimes it's best to have something not quite right in a hum so that everybody can say: 'Humph! I could have done it better myself.'"

"I couldn't have," said Christopher Robin quietly.

·CHAPTER NINE·

in which Tigger dreams of Africa

EYORE, THE OLD GREY DONKEY and ex-head master, had been working on his letters with the aid of broken sticks. He was now expert at the straight letters like A and E and F and H, but needed to find bendy sticks for the curvy ones like C and R and S.

"Then you can't make Christopher Robin," said Piglet, and added after a moment's thought: "Or Piglet."

"Or Eeyore," said Eeyore. "Can't make anything,

except THE. What good is THE without something to come after it?"

"None at all," said Piglet, who had come to see Eeyore just in case he hadn't heard Pooh's Cricketing Hum.

Eeyore looked down at Piglet's feet.

"I do appreciate this kind visit," he said, "but I'll thank you for not standing on my thistle patch. I'm running short."

"Should I help you look for some more?"

"If you have nothing better to do, Piglet. Old thistles are fine if you've got the teeth for 'em, but for crunchiness and fullness of flavour there is nothing to beat a patch of young thistles with the purple flowers still on them. What's more, little Piglet, they are a cure for aches and pains."

"Do you have some of those then, Eeyore?"

"After being wicket-keeper what can you expect?"

Just then, Lottie, who had been teasing the trout in the stream, which was sparkling and fresh again after a summer storm, joined them.

"Fine morning," she said pleasantly.

"No," said Eeyore. "It wasn't then, and it isn't now."

"Don't mind him," said Piglet. "He's out of thistles, Lottie."

"Is that all? I know where the best thistles are.

Would you like me to take you there, Eeyore?"

As they walked through the Forest carrying paper bags, a stripy thing bounced up to them.

"Good morning, Tigger," said Piglet nervously.

"No," said Eeyore. "It wasn't, and now it's getting worse."

"Hallo Piglet, hallo Eeyore, hallo Lottie," cried Tigger. "Where are you all off to?"

"We're looking for thistles for Eeyore's aches and pains," said Piglet.

"I shall come too!" Tigger bounced high over a tree stump and back.

"Could you not limit yourself to *small* bounces?" Lottie asked.

"Very small bounces," Eeyore warned.

"Like this!" said Piglet. He did a small bounce to show Tigger what he meant, and tripped over some bindweed.

The four of them set off. On the way, they met Kanga and Roo, who were enjoying the air after the storm, and the whole party headed into a cluster of trees.

Just inside, they passed a clump of blackberry bushes, heavy with succulent berries.

"Those are blackberries," said Lottie. "Best in a pie with shortcrust pastry and custard."

"Tiggers like blackberries," said Tigger, after tasting one.

"Well, be careful, Tigger," warned Kanga. "Only eat the black and juicy ones, and don't eat too many."

Tigger tasted several, and then grabbed a whole pawful, and then another and then another. As he munched, he said something which could have been: "Oommphph!" unless perhaps it was "Splurghfff!"

After a few swallows, Tigger beamed broadly and said: "Tiggers like blackberries very much," with which he grabbed another pawful.

Meanwhile, Eeyore had come to a copious clump of purple thistles and was chewing on one.

"Not the best," he mumbled as he chomped away, and grudgingly added: "Not the worst, either."

* * *

When Kanga, Tigger and Roo arrived home, Kanga said she would make them pancakes for dinner. But Tigger said that he didn't think he would be able to eat any pancakes, so Roo said that he would eat them for him – and he did. When the pancakes had been disposed of, there was Extract of Malt for afters, but Tigger said that he didn't think he could eat any of that either.

"Not even Extract of Malt?" asked Kanga. "My, my. That's what comes of snacks between meals!"

After dinner, Roo brought out the big atlas, which they had borrowed from Christopher Robin. While Kanga darned socks, Roo and Tigger jumped over oceans, conquered nations and tore off a corner of Madagascar by mistake.

Suddenly, Tigger sat back on his haunches, and looked down at West Africa, which was spread out beneath his feet. He blinked a couple of times, and let loose a magnificent burp.

"Tigger, dear!" said Kanga, a little less mildly than usual.

Roo started to giggle, then looked more closely at Tigger.

"Are you all right?" he asked.

"Never better!" said Tigger, burping again and looking startled. "What's that country?"

Looking over Tigger's shoulder, Kanga identified it: "That's the Ivory Coast."

"Ivory Coast," murmured Roo. "Sounds lovely."

Tigger said: "I was just wondering: where do I come from?"

"Don't you remember?" asked Kanga.

"Now you come to mention it, I do. I remember a forest, with trees much taller than the ones in the Hundred Acre Wood. And monkeys. I'm sure I remember monkeys. At least, I think I am sure."

"Sounds like Africa," said Kanga. "Now it's bath-time, and then bed."

"Oh no, not bath-time!" cried Roo, which was what he always said.

Tigger said nothing. Africa . . . Africa . . . it *sounded* right.

Tigger found he could not sleep. He tried lying on his back, but he did not know where to put his legs. He tried lying on his side, but his whiskers tickled. He tried standing up, but only Eeyore could sleep standing up, so finally he curled up in a corner under the ironing board and shut his eyes. But sleep would not come. His skin felt crawly, as if all his stripes were running into one big stripe, like raindrops on a windowpane, but, when he opened his eyes to check, he was not all orange or all black but just the same as he always was. He did not feel Tiggerish. He did not feel well. He burped and groaned. And, finally, he slipped into a fitful sleep.

Then he muttered: "Africa," but his eyes remained shut.

"I 'spect he's dreaming of the jungle," said Roo, when they found him the next morning, still muttering. "That's what I 'spect."

At midday, Kanga sent Roo with a message to Christopher Robin's house.

"Christopher Robin, Christopher Robin!" cried Roo. "Tigger's not well. He's twitching and making noises."

"What sort of noises?"

"Rude ones, mainly."

"It's probably influenza," said Christopher Robin. He had had it himself, and Matron had said to keep warm and drink lots. So he made a thermos of hot cocoa and took it around to Kanga's house, along with a blue blanket that had a silky bit around the edge.

"But I don't think he's cold," said Roo. "At least, he doesn't feel cold."

When Christopher Robin put the blanket over Tigger, he kicked it off, and when he poured out a mug of hot cocoa, Tigger sent it flying all over a woollen rug which a cousin of Kanga's had crocheted and sent her for Christmas.

Christopher Robin called on Rabbit and Owl.

Rabbit said: "Keep him warm and give him cocoa," which was not a lot of help, while Owl brought a black leather bag from which he removed a stethoscope, and listened to Tigger's chest.

"What can you hear?" asked Roo. "And can I be doctor next?"

"No," said Owl, "you cannot. All I can hear is drums, but it's probably just his heartbeat."

Tigger rolled his eyes and his tail stuck straight out behind him.

Just then, Pooh arrived, clutching a pot of honey.

"Do you think Tigger would like this?" he asked.

"Tiggers don't like honey," said Piglet.

"I had forgotten," said Pooh, and he smiled a small, relieved smile.

*   *   *

That night and all the next day, Tigger lay under the ironing board muttering to himself, watched over by each of his worried friends in turn. Then on the third day, when Rabbit was checking the tidiness of Kanga's cupboards while her back was turned, and going "tut-tut," Tigger got up and slipped outside.

"Poor Tigger," said Christopher Robin. "I wonder where he thinks he's going."

"To Africa, perhaps," said Pooh.

Roo asked: "Which way is Africa?"

But nobody seemed to know.

* * *

It was Eeyore who found Tigger, lying on his back under an oak, staring at the branches.

"Africa!" Tigger muttered reproachfully at the tree.

Eeyore lifted him gently onto his back and brought him home.

"I was not always very kind to him," the old donkey admitted, and sighed. "If only he hadn't *bounced*."

"He's still not well," said Piglet. "Look at how loose his skin is."

This was true. Tigger's skin appeared to be several sizes too large.

"His tongue is not a good colour," said Lottie. "I am not sure what colour it is meant to be, but I don't think it's that colour."

"It's meant to be tongue-coloured," Owl suggested. "And it is now the colour a tongue goes after it has eaten too many blackberries."

"Unripe, unwashed and without custard," added Lottie.

"I've been thinking," said Christopher Robin, "if I were poorly, what I would most want."

"To be well again," said Pooh.

"Yes, Pooh, but what else? I think I should like to be surrounded by friendly and familiar things."

"But he is," said Pooh.

"If he's decided he's African . . ."

Owl said, reasonably enough: "We can't carry him to Africa, he's too heavy. Unless . . . Eeyore?"

"Certainly not," said Eeyore.

"I wonder," said Christopher Robin. "Since we can't take him to Africa, then I wonder whether we could bring Africa to him."

"Africa!" said Tigger faintly, and burped.

Tigger lay in his favourite corner, restless and twitchy still, but in a kind of half-slumber. All around him

the others had been busy and now they were putting the finishing touches to what Christopher Robin had proposed.

At first Tigger was aware of a gentle drumming. Was it his heart? No, it was coming from outside him.

He opened his eyes. Where on earth could he be? Above him was a canopy of lush green branches, and around him were swathes of fern and mosses. Water was dripping from the leaves, and it was hot and steamy. There was even a hissing of snakes.

"Where am I?" asked Tigger in wonderment. "Could I be . . . could I really be in Africa?"

Then Christopher Robin's voice said: "Tigger, you are wherever you want to be. It's called imagination."

Tigger closed his eyes and fell happily asleep. Which was just as well, as it meant that he did not see Lottie drumming on two upturned waste-paper baskets with rolling pins belonging to Kanga and Rabbit, or Pooh up a ladder with a watering can, or Christopher Robin tending a fire, or even Roo blowing into the spouts of various kettles to make what he imagined might be snake-hisses.

From that moment, Tigger's slow recovery began. He began to do bending and stretching exercises, and his burps turned into occasional gentle hiccups. He demanded a spoonful of Extract of Malt every hour on the hour, and within a couple of days his skin no longer hung loose, his tongue was the pinkish colour proper for a fit Tigger, and his stripes – well, his stripes were the brightest and the best defined ever seen in the Hundred Acre Wood; possibly as bright as any in Africa.

*　　*　　*

One morning a week or so later, Roo and Tigger and Piglet were sliding down the water chute when

Christopher Robin and Pooh came briskly up to them. Christopher Robin was carrying a big book, and Pooh a sheet of handsome blue writing paper.

"Tigger," said Christopher Robin, "we have something important to tell you."

"Really?" said Tigger, and splashed water over Roo, who splashed water over Piglet, who splashed water over Tigger. "What's that?"

"You ought to be sitting down," said Christopher Robin. "It's sitting down stuff."

"Righty-ho!" said Tigger, and sat down twice with a bit of a bounce in between.

"Shall I tell him?" Pooh asked Christopher Robin, who nodded.

"Tigger, you aren't African!"

"'Course I am!" said Tigger.

"You can't be."

"Why can't I be?"

"You're a tiger and there aren't any tigers in Africa," Christopher Robin explained. "Tigers come from Asia. China and India and places like that."

"And circuses," said Pooh.

Tigger thought about all this for a moment. It was a good deal to take in.

"Who says?"

Christopher Robin opened the big book at a place he had marked with a slip of paper.

"The Encyclopedia does."

"Hmm . . ." Tigger considered this with his head on one side. Then he looked triumphantly at Pooh. "Bears don't come from England."

Christopher Robin smiled and said: "Well, there's one here, and there always will be. Pooh Bear."

"Am I the only one?" asked Pooh.

Christopher Robin thought for a moment.

"Well, maybe not the *only* bear in England," he concluded. "But in all the world you are the one and only, incomparable Winnie-the-Pooh."

·CHAPTER TEN·

*in which a Harvest Festival is held in the Forest
and Christopher Robin springs a surprise*

SUMMER WAS ALMOST OVER. The windfall apples lay on the ground, which was heavy with dew, and one morning there was mist curling in the hollows down by the stream.

Christopher Robin and Pooh were paying an Encouraging Visit to Eeyore, who was gloomier than ever. But after a few minutes Eeyore was showing no sign of being Encouraged, and his friends were running out of things to say.

"Did you know that it will soon be Harvest Festival?" asked Christopher Robin, after a particularly long silence.

"What's that then?" asked Eeyore suspiciously.

"Well, every September, people get together to celebrate the Gathering-in of the Crops," explained Christopher Robin. "They make corn dollies and collect produce and put it on display. Then they sing about everything being bright and beautiful."

"Is it?" Eeyore asked. "Can't say I'd noticed."

"What's produce?" asked Pooh.

"It's food that you've got spare, Pooh. Like a pot of honey."

"It is?" Pooh said, wondering if honey could be spare.

"Yes, and it ought to be the best pot. The idea is to give things to the Less Fortunate."

Pooh gulped, thinking of his row of honey jars, especially the pot second from the left at the back, which was the tallest and the fattest.

"Who are the Less Fortunate?" asked Pooh. He felt that he would be one of them, if he had to give away his honey.

"Well, I'm not sure," said Christopher Robin. He lay on his back, looking up at the sky with a thoughtful expression. "We could have a Harvest Festival here in the Forest," he said. "I could build a cart to put the produce in and tow it behind my bicycle. Then the Less Fortunate could see it and take things."

"You'll do as you like, of course," said Eeyore loudly, "but I'm not singing. Bad for the stomach."

*   *   *

Although Christopher Robin had learned carpentry at school, nobody had shown him how to make a cart, and it turned out to be quite tricky.

The wheels ended up rather squareish, and when he came to make the tyres there was no rubber, so he used a pair of old pyjamas instead. Then there was the

question of how to attach the cart to the chassis, and the chassis to the axle, and the axle to the wheels. Working all this out involved a lot of sitting around scratching his head and turning bits of wood over in his hands, but eventually the cart was finished. It was rather bumpy and hard to pull along, but a cart it certainly was.

Christopher Robin parked it in front of his house with a sign which read:

FOR PRODUSE. PUT IN HERE PLEEZ.

Once the animals had gathered around to admire the cart, everyone started to make suggestions for what else they could do to celebrate Harvest Festival. Kanga suggested baking cakes – always popular – and Rabbit suggested card games, like Snap, Old Maid and Racing Demon – not so popular, as Rabbit generally boasted when he won and sulked when he lost – but it was Christopher Robin who came up with a clever suggestion that would allow them to do all these things and more.

"It's a bit late in the summer," he said, "but why don't we have a fête? We could have blackberries and cream, instead of strawberries, and play games like Hoopla and Pin the Tail on the Donkey."

All the animals cheered – with the exception of Tigger, who thought he wouldn't eat any more blackberries, and Eeyore, who said: "Excuse me," with great dignity. Then he said it twice more until everyone else was quiet.

"I believe, Christopher Robin," he continued, "you will find that I already have a tail. True, it is attached by a nail, but you will understand my reluctance to have just anyone bashing away at it."

"Oh, Eeyore," said Christopher Robin. "I didn't mean you should . . ."

But the old donkey held up a hoof for silence. "I shall give rides to the little ones instead," he announced.

*   *   *

The morning of the Harvest Festival dawned bright and clear. Everyone had been planning and working for days, and by lunchtime the fête was set up. There were stalls selling the bric-a-brac that had turned up when Rabbit helped everyone clear out their houses and a hoopla game made from sticks and rings, and Owl's platform where he would stand to recite poetry and a mysterious booth made out of blankets hung over tree branches. 'HAVE YOUR PAW READ BY MADAME PETULENGRA' said a sign that was pinned to the outside.

In the middle of it all sat the cart, full of produce that gleamed in the September sunshine. There were haycorns from Piglet, a small pot of honey from Pooh, Strengthening Medicine from Tigger, home-made crab-apple jam from Rabbit, a whole tray of fairy cakes from Kanga and much, much more. It had all been decorated with heather and yellow gorse.

"Perfect," said Christopher Robin, looking around the glade when preparations were complete. "And now it's time for our picnic," he added, as one of the fairy cakes was grabbed from the cart by a baby rabbit.

The lunch was a fine one, with enough honeycomb and haycorns to suggest that perhaps not all the best

 produce had been set aside for the Less Fortunate. Then, as the sun started its journey down the other side of the sky, the animals opened their fête.

From the start, Piglet's hoopla stand was popular. It became especially busy when some of Rabbit's Friends and Relations decided to throw the rings over Piglet instead of over the pegs. Things only calmed down again when Tigger got a ring

wedged around his head and Christopher Robin had to remove it with soapy water.

The mysterious blanket booth turned out to contain Lottie, seated in a rocking chair and wearing a mauve turban. If you paid her a small coin and offered her your paw to examine, she would tell you either that you would cross the water or that you would meet with a handsome

stranger. If you paid her a large coin, you found out you were going to do both at the same time.

Meanwhile, Eeyore tramped slowly around the glade, with a crowd of little rabbits clinging to his back, shrieking with laughter.

Then, when you tired of these wonderful things, you could go to Rabbit's card booth and find yourself obliged to lose at various different games. Or you could

listen to Owl reciting Uncle Robert's favourite poem, but it was a very long poem and when it came to the hard-to-remember bits, Owl flapped his wings a few times and said "etcetera," "and so forth," "and so on" in such a grand way that it was really just as good as the poem. Or you could do as Pooh did, and wander around from stall to stall, marvelling at everything, trying all the games, and not doing terribly well at anything, except at rolling the penny.

And so the celebrations went on all afternoon, until Kanga announced that, Harvest Festival or not, it was time for Roo to go home to bed.

"But it won't be dark for hours," protested Roo.

"Now, I've told you –" started Kanga.

But Pooh wasn't listening to this. He was looking around the glade, for something that wasn't there.

"Where is Christopher Robin?" he asked.

Everybody stopped what they were doing.

Rabbit looked from side to side, and said: "He isn't here."

"I know where he isn't," said Pooh, "but there's still a lot of other places he might be."

"We must Organdise a Search Party!" squeaked Roo excitedly.

"No, dear," said Kanga, "because then we might all get lost instead of just Christopher Robin."

"He isn't lost," said Piglet, sounding as if he wasn't quite sure. "We don't know where he is, but that isn't the same thing at all. Christopher Robin is just on his own somewhere. I wonder if that means he wants to be on his own . . . Oh dear."

It was then that Owl, whose eyesight was the best, flew up above the tallest of the tall oaks. But even with his sharp eyes there was no Christopher Robin to be seen.

Eeyore looked around the remains of the fête and sniffed. "Well then," he said, "if that's the end of that, I'd better be going." But he did not leave.

"Roo, dear, it really is time for bed!" said Kanga, her voice becoming quite sharp.

But nobody moved.

Pooh kept looking at the cart and the pot of honey. He was sure he had seen Tigger helping himself to a gulp or two of the Strengthening Medicine, and Piglet retrieving one or five of the finest haycorns. So he thought to himself that there was no harm in having just a little taste of the honey.

By the time he was on to his ninth or tenth taste, he could hear a faint clunking and clattering sound. He looked around at the others, and they were all listening too.

"That sounds like a bicycle," he said.

"And if it's a bicycle," said Piglet, "there must be somebody on it to do the pedalling, and the only one who isn't here is Christopher Robin, and he's the only one with a bicycle."

Piglet was quite correct. It was Christopher Robin's bicycle and Christopher Robin was riding it.

Everyone breathed a sigh of relief when Christopher Robin came rattling into the glade on his bicycle. He jumped off and leaned it against a tree.

"Sorry I left the party, but I wanted to fetch you a little surprise," he explained.

From his bicycle basket, he took some large objects that were carefully wrapped in old jerseys. They turned out to be the gramophone and a box of records. The animals watched as he unwrapped them and set them down on the grass.

"I thought we could finish the day with some dancing," he said cheerfully. "Then I will take your generous presents to the Less Fortunate."

Christopher Robin glanced into the cart, and then peered inside more closely.

"Or maybe I won't," he added. Then he leant over the gramophone to wind the handle, and finished quietly: "Anyway, I'm leaving this here for you."

Then the loudest, jumpiest, most harmonious and tumultuous music came tumbling out of the gramophone horn – and nobody could stay still.

Shake your feathers
Move your feet about
For I'm sweet about you.
Feel the beat because
I'm incomplete because
I am lost without you.

They danced a proper Hundred Acre Wood dance this time. At first it owed something to Lottie's dancing class, but then it became wilder, with much leaping up into the air. Tigger and Kanga vied to see who could jump highest – the results were pretty even – and Roo and Piglet vied to see who could crouch down lowest – they were both beaten by Henry Rush, who hurried into a clump of heather immediately afterwards, for fear of being trodden on. And even Eeyore danced, a dance all his own, with flying hooves and mane and loud braying and his tail going here, there and everywhere.

After *Shake Your Feathers*, they played *The Bam Bam Bammy Shore* and *Yes, We Have No Bananas* and *My Grandfather's Clock*. And while *The Bam Bam Bammy Shore* was playing for the second time, Christopher Robin stopped dancing, and rolled up the jerseys, and put them in the basket of his bicycle.

Pooh, who was by now rather tired, left the dance as well. He padded over to see what Christopher Robin was doing, although he thought he could guess.

"Ah," said Pooh solemnly, because this was one of those moments when you had to say something, even though nothing was quite right for the occasion.

"Well then, Pooh," said Christopher Robin, leaning his bicycle back against the tree.

"So . . ."

He stopped to give Pooh a hug. It was a bit awkward, because Christopher Robin was quite tall these days, but Pooh hugged him back as best he could.

Over Pooh's head, Christopher Robin finished: "I'll be away for a while again, but I know you'll look after the Forest."

"I'll try," said Pooh. Really, he wasn't sure what Looking After the Forest might involve. But if Christopher Robin thought he could do it, that meant that he could.

Christopher Robin let go and gave Pooh a nod. He got on his bicycle and pedalled swiftly away, turning just once to give a last wave and a smile before he was lost among the trees.

* * *

Later, after Owl and Rabbit had had an argument over who would look after the gramophone and the records, and Lottie and Eeyore had solved the argument by carrying off the whole lot between them, Pooh and Piglet walked home through the moonlit wood.

"I wonder why things have to change," murmured Piglet.

Pooh thought for a while, then said: "It gives them a chance to get better. Like when the bees went away, and came back."

"I suppose so," said Piglet, a bit hesitantly. Then he cheered up. "It's been a good summer, really. Do you remember that six I hit to win the cricket match?"

"I do," said Pooh, a bit less cheerfully than Piglet, as he also remembered being hit on the nose by the cricket ball. And he remembered Piglet going down the well, and the Census, and the Academy, and the produce and the gramophone. It all seemed mixed up with the fluff in his head, but at the same time it was so special that it deserved a hum. So he sat down on a log and made one up.

> Christopher Robin has gone away.
> He would not stay, no, he would not stay.
> When will we see him? Will he be back?
> Did he even have time to pack?

> He left his music, but took his machine,
> The best and the bluest we'd ever seen.
> He left us all wondering: Gone for good?
> No! He'll be back to our lovely wood.

> One day perhaps when the sun is high,
> Out of the blue we will hear him cry:
> "Piglet and Eeyore, Rabbit and Pooh,
> I'm back again to spend time with you."

"I've singed it, but I haven't signed it," said Pooh, "because I can't write."

"Doesn't matter," said Piglet. "I was worried you weren't going to put me in like you always used to. But then at the end you did."

"You don't rhyme with very much," said Pooh.

"Are there many rhymes for Christopher Robin?" wondered Piglet.

"I don't think so. Not good ones."

"We could go and ask him tomorrow."

Then they remembered that Christopher Robin wouldn't be there tomorrow, or the next day.

So off they went, together. And if you pass by the Hundred Acre Wood on an early autumn evening, you might see them, arm in arm, strolling contentedly under the trees, until they are swallowed up by the mist.

Winnie-the-Pooh

Also available to collect in Hardback and Paperback

  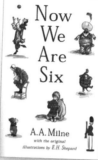 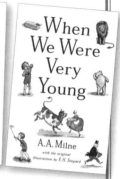

Winnie-the-Pooh

978 1 4052 2398 0 (hb)   978 1 4052 1116 1 (pb)

£12.99   £6.99

The House at Pooh Corner

978 1 4052 2995 1 (hb)   978 1 4052 1117 8 (pb)

£12.99   £6.99

Now We Are Six

978 1 4052 2993 7 (hb)   978 1 4052 1119 2 (pb)

£9.99   £6.99

When We Were Very Young

978 1 4052 2994 4 (hb)   978 1 4052 1118 5 (pb)

£9.99   £6.99

Winnie-the-Pooh

Gift collections to treasure

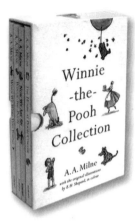

Winnie-the-Pooh Collection
Four paperback editions in an elegant slipcase

978 1 4052 1120 8

£25.00

Winnie-the-Pooh
The Complete Collection of Stories and Poems
A hardback compilation with slipcase cover

978 0 4161 9961 1

£29.99